One Summer in Tuscany

Annie Seaton

This is a work of fiction. Characters, institutions and organisations mentioned in this novel are either the product of the author's imagination or, if real, used fictitiously without any intent to describe actual conduct.

ISBN 9781923048119

Dedication

I dedicate this story to the group of wonderful women who attended the writing workshop with me in Tuscany in June 2014, with a special mention for Eloisa James who taught us so much. Wonderful lessons, fabulous company and lifelong connections, not to mention the gelati!

Also by Annie Seaton

Standalone Books
Whitsunday Dawn
Undara
Osprey Reef
East of Alice
Porter Sisters Series
Kakadu Sunset
Daintree
Diamond Sky
Hidden Valley
Larapinta
Kakadu Dawn

Others
Four Seasons Short and Sweet
Deadly Secrets
Adventures in Time
Silver Valley Witch
The Emerald Necklace
An Aussie Christmas Duo
Follow the Sun
Ten days in Paradise

Pentecost Island Series
Pippa
Eliza
Nell
Tamsin
Evie
Cherry
Odessa
Sienna
Tess
Isla

The House on the Hill series
Beach House
Beach Music
Beach Walk
Beach Dreams

Sunshine Coast Series
Waiting for Ana
The Trouble with Jack
Healing His Heart

Second Chance Bay Series
Her Outback Playboy
Her Outback Protector
Her Outback Haven
Her Outback Paradise
The McDougalls of Second Chance Bay
Richards Brothers Series
The Trouble with Paradise
Marry in Haste
Outback Sunrise

Love Across Time Series
Come Back to Me
Follow Me
Finding Home
The Threads that Bind
Love Across Time 1-4 Boxed Set

Bindarra Creek
Worth the Wait
Full Circle
Secrets of River Cottage
Bindarra Creek Duo
A Clever Christmas
The Augathella Girls Series
Outback Roads
Outback Sky
Outback Escape
Outback Wind
Outback Dawn
Outback Moonlight
Outback Dust
Outback Hope

An Augathella Surprise
An Augathella Baby
...and more to come.

Chapter One

Nic Baldini held the phone to his ear with one hand, wondering what his younger brother wanted as he turned the key in the massive door.

'Another month, bro.' His younger brother, Antonio's voice held suppressed excitement.

The front door of the villa groaned as Nic pushed it open; the wooden door held eight rows of metal studs in a regular pattern from top to bottom. The studs were first used on external doors and gates as protection from the swords and axes of enemy attacks. When he was a child, they had come to the Baldini medieval villa for the summer holidays; it was too draughty and cold in the winter. The stories of medieval battles had fascinated Nic, and he and Antonio had staged their mock battles.

'Are you still there, Nic?'

'Sorry, yes. I was looking at the door.'

'What door? Are you listening to me?'

Nic stepped inside and stood observing the wide foyer in front of him. 'The villa. Yes, it's disappointing, but I suppose a month works. It'll be that long before I'm back in Florence. So why so upbeat? What inside info have you got?'

'You're the favourite for the position. There's a guy from Sweden who supports upcoming artists, but they say you have the edge.'

'They?' Nic tried to focus on the conversation as a burst of colour met his eyes.

Antonio had his finger on the pulse in the city. Most of the women he dated—and they were many—had connections to the higher echelons of Florentine society.

'Isabella for one. She's executive assistant to the director of the Uffizi Gallery.'

Nic turned his back to the room. 'So, she thinks I'm in?'

'Very close. If you can just do something to show you're prepared to keep sponsoring local artists. Apparently, there was some speculation that your focus on the children's charity may have replaced your interest in the art scene.'

'How much will it take?'

'Uh-uh. Not money this time. Your recent protégées haven't had successful shows, and the word is you may be moving on to other interests. You need a show that gets the crowd talking.' Antonio's voice was muffled as he spoke to someone else. 'Have to go, Nic. But listen. Don't worry. It should be okay. If I hear anything more, I'll call. But think about it.'

'Will do. But that's all. No work calls.'

'Okay.'

Nic ended the call and lifted his gaze to the amazing room surrounding him. He'd bought *Casa Marmo* from his father's company three years ago, but unfortunately hadn't spent anywhere near the time here he'd hoped to. This was the first time he'd seen the changes himself; he'd supervised the renovations from afar over the past year, and the photographs he'd been emailed as the work progressed hadn't done justice to the improvements in the building that had stood in this spot—owned by the Baldini family—since the sixteenth century. He'd insisted on keeping the original metal-studded door. Who knew? One day he might have sons who'd be as fascinated with the history of the building as he was. But there was no time for that yet. Nic was too busy with his philanthropic activities and his career in the family marble business since his father had supposedly retired.

He slowly walked towards the salon, extremely pleased with the changes the builders from Florence had wrought; the place looked incredible. They had followed his instructions to the letter and Nic was more than happy with the changes he'd sent via email before he'd come down for this, his third annual visit since he'd moved back to Italy from New York. The original wide tiles in the foyer had been repaired and re-grouted. A row of glittering chandeliers, the pendants sending rainbows of light to the walls as they caught the afternoon sun, defined the wide room that led from the huge entrance foyer to the salon.

As he bent down and ran his fingers across the smooth surface of the pristine white marble stand near the doorway of the formal dining room, peace filtered through Nic; he would do everything he could to make this venture successful. He'd put aside his original plan to solely build a retreat for the established artists he took on as protégées because he'd been let down too many times.

Why was it that they always saw the money and didn't get that he was trying to help them grow further?

It was disillusioning. No more. It was time to focus on his art in different ways. To focus on those young students who had their careers ahead of them and were prepared to focus on their art . . . and not what he could do for them. He'd wasted too much time, energy *and* money, trying to discover the next big name. But he wanted that board position more than anything, and Antonio's call had been encouraging. If this month turned out as he hoped, he would walk away from Baldini Enterprises and devote his time to philanthropic endeavours.

But he would think about that later.

He turned away from the window and walked back through the sun-filled room. Keeping with the original design, the archways and walls were painted a rich terracotta. Small tables were placed beside the enticingly-soft sofas. The caretaker had even placed fresh lilacs in the antique vases, bringing the scent of the garden into the open space. The eastern wall had been ripped out and replaced with sliding glass doors opening to the incredible view of the vineyards below. Beyond the vineyards on the back acreage, the old stables had been converted into a block of light-filled studios, ready for the first group of young art students who would be here later this summer. As a benefactor to three of the art schools in Florence, this project was close to his heart.

Not for the first time since returning to Tuscany, Nic thought of his mother. She would have appreciated the changes to the villa and been delighted to see him back in Tuscany. And she would have been proud of the philanthropic work he was doing with the young artists. She'd be down here with them making coffee, entertaining them when they were painting, and most importantly encouraging their talent. Mamma had been the one to foster Nic's artistic side. She'd made him promise that every year, he'd come here leaving behind the stress of running the business, and devoting his time to indulging his dream. It had taken him five years after her death to honour his promise. He was thirty; it was past time. Now this summer in Tuscany would be spent following that dream, and he would keep her memory alive.

But she was gone.

He pushed away the pain and continued upstairs. When he entered his bedroom, he stopped in his tracks. The finer details of the decor had been left in the hands of Alessandro, one of the top designers in Rome, and the builder had been given carte blanche, but the ornate mirrors on each wall were not what Nic had expected. Shaking his head, he turned slowly and smiled. Alessandro had succeeded with this room, too. Rather than being tacky, the gilded mirrors lent a studied elegance to the large room. He walked over to the bed that was strewn with dozens of cushions in jewel-like colours, and sat on the scarlet cover, his reflection grinning back at him. Yes, it was superb, but this room was more suited to a harem than a Tuscan villa. A decadent but wasted sentiment. He didn't want company in this house—not this trip anyway; it would interfere with the painting he intended to do.

Nic stood and moved across to the window that overlooked the Arno Valley. The road into the villa was lined with century-old pine trees and they swayed gently in the early evening breeze. As he stared down at the view that his mother had loved so much, the pain of her loss clung to him like the mist that hovered around the blue hills in the distance.

The villa sprawled down the hill only a couple of miles south of the village of Castellina-in-Chianti. An adjacent building—previously the old servant's quarters—had been converted into a retreat for children who were recovering from illness and the first group would also be here in the autumn. Nic was also a benefactor of the children's hospital in Florence; the project had been his idea.

So here I am.

Antonio could take care of the export side of the business for the summer. Nic didn't intend to think about work at all. Usually, when the rest of Italy shut down in the heat, he worked and this reprieve was long overdue.

Finally, he turned and stepped back into the wide hall, hesitating at the final door before taking a deep breath and pushing open the ornately carved door into the studio he had designed himself.

Again, a surge of pleasure filled him. Every instruction had been carried out to the last detail. The newly closed-in room was magnificent and ready for him to begin painting. Last week, Nic had hired an art supplier in Siena to supply and set up his art equipment for him.

A smile crossed his face as he turned to the blank canvas waiting on the easel beside the window. For the few weeks, he was going to indulge himself, forget business, and imagine what his life would have been like if he'd followed his passion and not the path of family duty his father had mapped out for him.

Forget the details of the export business deals and the issues at the quarry and indulge the creative muse that had consumed him for as long as he could remember. He pulled off his shirt and rubbed his hands together as he crossed to the table where the paints were laid out. For the first time in a long time, he was going to be the Nic Baldini he wanted to be. An artist, not a businessman.

##

Half an hour later, Nic's satisfaction, and confidence that he could be the person he wanted had disappeared. The canvas was white; still a blank surface in front of him and his paints remained untouched. He stood in front of the easel, frustration building as he stared at the empty canvas. Finally, in disgust, he threw the sable brush to the table and crossed the large open space to the door.

I'm tired. That's all it is.

The business meeting in the States had been a difficult one, the flight from New York to Rome, and then the drive back to Carrara before he'd headed south again this afternoon to the villa had made for a long couple of days. That's all it was; he was overtired. As Nic reached the doorway, he caught sight of his reflection in the mirror positioned across from the window. His tattoo stood out in sharp relief against his skin; pale from spending the winter in his office overlooking the quarry.

Coraggio. The simple word in a black fancy-flowing script was centred on his chest. And the base of each 'g' was formed by the legs of the Cancerian crab. Part of his rebellion against his father's denial of his dream; Papa had refused to allow him to go to art school and had sent him to Carrara to work in the quarry the summer before he began his business degree.

On his return to Florence, he had begged again, but to no avail. Mamma had smiled sweetly and hugged him in her usual vague way. Nic stared through the window as the memories flitted through his mind. He watched a farmer cutting hay on the hill across from the villa. Lazy spirals of smoke rose in the sky from the small cottages scattered around the valley. When she was dying, Mamma had told him that he would be happy without her and that she had no doubt he would one day follow his true path in life but his father had apparently never received such comfort from her. His father had never managed to work through the grief of losing her and was a shell of the man he had once been.

Nic had been so angry about not going to art school, his mother had taken him for a drive into the Tuscan countryside to meet an old friend who lived in a small village south of Florence. She had ignored his teenage moodiness most of the time. Mamma would simply smile and pull out her astrological charts and nod sagely and point to the crab. To make her happy he'd gone along with the reading of his palm and the compilation of his chart by his mother's friend, a gypsy woman. He'd ignored their mutterings about moons and planets rising, but his surly mood had disappeared when the woman with the cloud of black hair had asked if she could tattoo his path onto his chest. He could still remember her coal-black eyes burning into his as she'd read his palm, and her mutterings about him finding his destiny in this very countryside.

Nic grinned at the memory. He'd managed to hide the tattoo from his father for six months—courage hadn't kicked in yet—and when his father had noticed it, Nic had almost been disinherited. Art school had looked promising for a while, but his father had been preoccupied with managing the quarry, using his career to fill the void in his life after the death of his wife. Nic swore he would never tie himself to one person like that. He would never suffer grief the way his father had. Papa forgot about the tattoo, and in a strange way, it reinforced Nic's desire to draw on his courage to face life and all that it threw at him. Nic had followed "the plan" and gone to university and into the family business which had grown into one of the top marble export companies in Italy. But the word was a constant reminder to him to stay true to his beliefs and rely on no one, no matter what the world threw at him.

Corragio. It was emblazoned on his chest and had helped

him cope with his mother's death. And to put up with the way his father treated him.

All he needed now before he immersed himself in his art was a meal and a good night's sleep. The muse would come back tomorrow.

Corragio.

Grabbing his black shirt and slipping it back on, he went downstairs, picked up his car keys and pulled the door to the villa closed behind him.

Chapter Two

Gia Carelli slammed the door shut, grabbed her bicycle from the wall next to the old sink where her paint brushes soaked in a dozen glass bottles, and pushed it to the gate. As the tyres crunched over the loose white stones on the narrow path a loud pop came from the back.

'*Dio*, no.' She groaned as she looked down at the old bicycle. The back tyre was quickly going flat. She squeezed her eyes shut and hoped that when she opened them maybe she'd imagined it. The same wide brown eyes as her father's, but Papa's would be filled with the usual disappointment when she was late for work at the family restaurant. Gia had been immersed in her painting and had lost track of the time—as she always did. Of course, when she'd looked for her work clothes, they were all in the laundry basket—dirty. She picked up the set she'd worn last night, pulled her skirt around and twisted it to the side so the sauce stain was almost hidden. Shaking out the crumpled shirt, she rolled her eyes. Sometimes, she wondered why she bothered No matter what she did, she never measured up to her family's expectations. They treated her with kid gloves and tried to make her happy, but they just didn't *understand* her. If it was up to her parents she'd be happily married to some nice

Italian boy from their village and raising a tribe of *bambinos*.

Gia shivered. She couldn't think of anything worse. Being the baby of the family made life so hard.

The tyre was definitely going flat. And on closer inspection, there was a huge cut in the rubber. So, she couldn't even pump it up enough to get down the hill in time for work. She would have to buy a whole new tyre.

Gia gripped the bike as frustration took hold; breathing in slowly she stared at the scarlet roses tumbling from the roof of the old shed, trying to calm herself. The colour was exactly what she'd been trying to mix last night but the light from the hanging light bulb in her studio at the back of the old cottage had been too weak. Painting through the night, after being on her feet waitressing late into the evening, just didn't work. Her art was her life, her passion—if only her family understood that, they would realise she was not a meek and shy young woman who needed protection. The problem was, she needed money for rent, although if Mamma had her way, Gia would be back in the family home and not "wasting" time painting flowers.

They just didn't understand the need that drove her. Art wasn't a choice; it was what defined her. Her paintings and the time she spent creating them were as essential to her as the air she breathed.

No matter how much she hated it, Gia had to work in the

family business. It was just the way it was and what was expected of her. And, yes, that notion sounded as old as the buildings in the village square, but such was the way of life in her little corner of the world. Her parents meant well. Truly, they did. At times she could smile at their ways; it was the way they had been brought up and was all they knew.

But they didn't know *her*. There was no way they would support her art. Her art was as necessary to her as the air she breathed, but did they understand that?

Not a chance. According to Papa, he was "helping" her with a job in the family restaurant and he was always on the lookout for a suitable husband for Gia to bring into the Carelli family. What he was doing was crushing her dream, slowly and surely with every hour that she spent serving tables.

As soon as she'd saved enough from waitressing, she was out of this quaint little village in Tuscany where she'd grown up. And if working in the family restaurant was the only way she'd get enough money together to escape to the Santa Reparata International School of Art in Florence, she'd just put up with it. As much as she would have loved to have had a show to sell some of her landscapes to save more, not only couldn't she afford it, Gia didn't have the confidence to show her work publicly. That's why she had to go to Florence and study her craft. She had to be better, and studying was the only way to improve her skill.

She looked at the cheap watch on her wrist—the watch her brother, Gabriel had bought so she would *not* be late for work—and sighed. If she was late—again—it would be more ammunition for Papa to get her to move back home where she would be *safe*.

Pfft. Didn't they realise that at twenty-three she was more than ready to leave the nest and was quite capable of looking after herself? Ever since she'd suffered a debilitating bout of glandular fever in her early teens, her parents had been overprotective. She'd recovered completely and now was healthy and as strong as a horse, but no . . . Papa still considered her his delicate little flower.

Gabriel had already called this afternoon to remind her not to be late—the restaurant was full to capacity. She knew there'd be no disappointment in *his* eyes; her brother would be coldly angry.

'You worry too much,' she'd said, trying to diffuse his temper. 'I'll be there and I'll work as late as you need me.'

She had eleven minutes to get there. Eleven minutes on a bike as antiquated as the village, and with a half-flat tyre. She *could* walk. Damn it, she'd walk ten times that distance over the next few hours. But she was *not* going to be late. The bike would have to get her there, deflating tyre and all.

Gia opened the gate and pushed the bike out onto the road. She ignored the way the light played on the olive trees across the road as a silver ray of sunshine poured down on the top of the hill. But she stored it in her memory as her gaze lingered on the trees.

Oh no, the olives! She was supposed to pick up the olives for the restaurant from Uncle Luigi.

No time to get the olives. Gabriel will be angry. The words ran around Gia's mind in time with the wheels as she pumped the pedals and rode up the slight incline towards the village. Once she reached the top of the first hill and headed down to the bottom, the bike whizzed along the cobblestones, past olive groves and vineyards, toward the final hill before the village. She stood and pushed the pedals down hard as she neared the crest, the muscles in her calves screaming with the effort. Thank God, she was fit from running around the restaurant. As the road narrowed on the final curve Gia could see the parking lot at the back of the old stone building that housed the restaurant. Cars lined both sides of the grass, the spaces were almost full and it was only early. That meant a busy night ahead. At least time would go fast.

When she cleared the crest, Gia turned for a second, looking down over her shoulder to see how the tyre was holding up.

Good. Still a quarter full of air. As she turned back to face the road ahead, a horn blared from her left. Instinctively she cut to the right side of the road, bouncing over the kerb and narrowly managing not to tumble over the handlebars. The half-flat tyre wobbled precariously, and she jumped off the bike as soon as she reached the grass verge.

A low-slung sports car pulled up, centimetres away from her legs. She pressed herself against the still-warm stone and groaned when her shirt caught on a protruding brick. The anger that had been simmering in her chest ever since she'd had to put her paintbrush aside and leave for work, finally boiled over.

She shook her fist at the driver. '*Idiota.*' Folding her arms, she watched as he climbed out of the car.

No, not climbed. More like he uncoiled himself from the car and walked over to her, his face etched into a frown.

'Hey, calm down.' He held his hands up as he spoke. Olive skin against a black button-down shirt filled her vision. Summer was coming and the road was full of damned tourists roaring through their village. All right, so not every tourist was as attractive as this and she couldn't help her eyes running over the long lean body and gorgeous . . . Gia pulled her thoughts back to her predicament and glared at him.

'Watch where you are driving! This road is narrow and you shouldn't be speeding.'

'You shouldn't have been in the middle of the road with your back to oncoming traffic.' His voice was deep and gentle, and his words were tinged with a regional accent. Sunshades covered his eyes and Gia couldn't see his expression. 'It was just as well I was paying attention to the road.'

For Gia, it was the last straw. Her shirt was torn—she could feel the cool breeze through the rip in the cotton. She would be late for work. Her father would sigh and Gabriel would yell at her. The frustration of leaving a half-done landscape, because she'd had to leave to go to the restaurant, added to her temper.

This guy in his fancy car, with his perfectly pressed fancy clothes and his designer sunshades sitting above perfectly-shaven cheeks, leaned over her and the smell of some ridiculously expensive—well, she was sure it would be—cologne washed over her.

It all combined to tip her over the edge. She shoved her finger into the guy's chest. Into the perfectly pressed shirt. And looked up into that perfect face. 'Well, *signore*, you should watch where you're going *all* of the time.' She turned and gestured to the muddy path that she now stood on. '*I* had no choice.'

One at a time, she lifted her feet carefully from the sticky mud and stepped back onto the road. Gia turned her back to the car, and to the driver, with a final comment thrown over her shoulder. 'So, before you start your fancy car, please let me get safely around the corner.'

Knowing her tone was impolite, she headed off, resisting the urge to look back at him. She hadn't seen such a good-looking man for a long time. The muscles she had felt beneath his shirt had been perfectly sculpted. He would be beautiful to paint.

She pushed the thought away. If she could keep her temper fired, she'd be able to put up with her brother's inevitable anger. If Gabriel said one thing about her being late, he could find another waitress for the night.

And pigs might fly. She would never speak to her family like she'd just spoken to this stranger. Maybe she should. It had felt good to say what she really thought, for once in her life.

Chapter Three

Nic watched the retreating back of the little spitfire who'd just poked him in the chest. He could have been equally rude back to her—he'd been cruising slowly down the road into the village, not speeding——but he'd never be rude to a woman. Despite her rather dramatic tirade, he didn't react. Nothing was going to interfere with his happiness over the summer. This was his first night of being incommunicado from the world of business. He could start painting in the morning. And best of all, he'd just had a text from Ben, his personal assistant, to say that two more companies had taken up the challenge to match his million-dollar donation to *l'Ospedalino*, the children's hospital in Florence.

So, one little madam with a bad attitude, dressed in torn and crumpled clothes, had no chance of ruining his evening. He touched the spot on his chest where she'd poked him, right on his tattoo. Funny, how he'd just been thinking of Mamma's gypsy friend. This young woman had reminded him of her, the woman who had given him his tattoo. The little firebrand who had just disappeared around the corner was much younger than the tattoo artist but she had the same jet-black hair and dark, flashing eyes.

Beautiful eyes, even when they'd been flashing anger. It

was that spark of anger he'd admired most. The hint of passion that spoke of a complexity in the young woman. It . . . intrigued him.

Her black curls had been pulled back into a messy ponytail, but a few stray strands had hung untidily across her face. Her clothes were crumpled and there was a smear of dirt on her cheek near the edge of the square black glasses that framed her eyes. It was unusual to see a gypsy so far from the city these days. Most of them hung around the train station in Florence and at the city tourist attractions, looking to scam unsuspecting visitors. But Nic shouldn't make assumptions. Although when he'd come around the curve, she'd been riding quickly along the road—maybe she'd done something she shouldn't have and was trying to get away?

He shrugged as he climbed back into the Morgan Roadster 3.7 which he'd driven down from Florence that afternoon. The owner of the car dealership had been more than happy to let him take it for his trip; the Baldinis were one of their biggest accounts. The reviews of the car he'd read had been right; the Roadster had performed so well he was going to call Ben when he got back, and tell him to lease it for the company fleet. Now, a meal at Giannino's restaurant in Castellina, and a couple of glasses of fine wine and he could contemplate the subject for his painting.

Life was good.

Nic drove further up the road and then turned the compact, but powerful, car onto the sloping driveway of the restaurant. He parked in the last vacant spot on the grass at the rear of the building and stood beside the car for a moment looking out over the valley. The Tuscan hills in the distance held a bluish tinge as the mist settled in the early summer evening. His fingers itched to paint the scene.

Unusual. Landscapes weren't really his thing. So many reproductions of Tuscan landscapes filled the tourist shops and the *Piazza della Repubblica* in Florence that Nic preferred to paint more detailed still life abstracts, and portraits. If his father hadn't pushed him into an MBA so he could take a hands-on role in the family marble business, Nic would spend more time painting and not focusing on business twenty-four-seven.

That was the problem with being the eldest son. If it had been up to him, he would indulge himself with his art every day and not just during the time he allowed himself each summer. This year he was staying for a month. Antonio could run the business. Nic would be quite happy to hand it over to his younger brother. He huffed out a breath. Who was he kidding? Each summer he imagined what his life would have been like if he'd become an artist but he knew he'd miss the cut and thrust of the business if he handed it over to Antonio. Everything he did was with a single-minded focus—the month would be focused on his art. And then back to the heady world of business, after his days of self-indulgence.

Nic needed to be in control of every aspect of his life and was well aware that the death of his mother and watching his strong father flounder as he tried to deal with his grief played a role in the way he lived his own life. He made sure there was no chance of such a devastating loss for him; he gained his pleasure and satisfaction with his charity work although lately he had been jaded by those who saw his philanthropic work as an entrée to the family's wealth.

Nic frowned, chasing away the thoughts of work. No more for a month. As well as painting, it would be good to take a break from people who tried to befriend him as soon as they heard the Baldini name. From now on, he'd asked Ben to set up the charity work under another company so it appeared as though there was no connection with him. And for this holiday, he was simply Nic, visiting the beautiful Tuscan countryside and having his creative muse kick back into action.

He crossed the empty outdoor dining area. The umbrellas were up but the tables were empty because of the light rain that had fallen when the brief storm had passed through the valley. A buzz of noise met him as he stepped into the foyer of the restaurant. Luckily, he'd called ahead for a reservation. He hadn't tried out *Giannino's* since he'd bought the villa from his father. Nic had spent his first two visits to the place enjoying the solitude, but tonight his frustration at the muse deserting him had resulted in him taking the car out for a spin and trying some of the local cuisine before he shut himself away from the world.

The *maître d'* met him at the door and ushered him through the packed tables, past the buffet to a small table tucked into an alcove between a staircase and a large window that looked out over the scene he'd been admiring only minutes before. Nic took an appreciative breath as he looked around; fine aromas drifted through the restaurant. A wood-fired pizza oven was set just inside the main door, and another narrow doorway across the room looked like it led down into a cellar. Light glinted off the racks of wine that lined the walls to waist height on each side of a staircase leading downstairs. Another staircase near his table led upstairs, and from the noise drifting down, it sounded like there was a crowd up there, too. A sign that the food would be good. The *maitre d'* pulled out the chair for him and then gestured to the other chair. 'Or perhaps you would prefer to look at the view?'

Nic shook his head. 'This will be fine, thank you.'

He sat and the young man flicked the napkin over his lap and passed him the wine list. 'Welcome. My name is Gabriel, and I hope you enjoy your evening at our family restaurant.'

Gabriel was immaculately dressed; a sharp crease in his trousers and a snowy white apron covered his bright yellow shirt. 'Would you prefer sparkling or still water while you wait, *signore?*'

'*Acqua frizzante, per favore.*' Nic looked down at the menu after Gabriel left. The selection was equal to the best restaurants he frequented when he was in Florence. When he was at home in his apartment in Carrara and he had time, Nic enjoyed cooking for himself. But with the long hours he spent at the quarry or in business meetings, there was never enough time to indulge in his love of cooking—just like his art. This summer would be for him—for doing the things he loved, with not one thought given to the business. Antonio was the only one who knew where he was and his brother knew not to contact him unless something dire happened.

Nic looked at the menu, but the sound of raised voices coming from the small alcove at the base of the stairs caught his attention. A red velvet curtain hid one of the speakers from his view but he could see the yellow shirt of the young man who had seated him. The young man waved his arms and his head bobbed with each word as if to emphasise his obvious displeasure. '*Non solo sei in ritardo . . . Ma . . . dimenticavo . . . papà . . . sconvolto.*'

Snatches of the conversation reached him and Nic lowered his head back to the menu. *Not only are you late but someone's father was going to be upset.* Staff problems; Nic knew all about them. But as long as they didn't impact his meal, he didn't care.

'You look like a . . . a hoyden.' Gabriel's voice was louder. 'Now go and tidy your hair and wash that paint from your face.'

'I'm sorry. If you don't want me tonight, I can go home.' The soft voice trembled and Nic frowned. The poor waitress sounded as if she was on the verge of tears. If there was one thing Nic could not abide it was bullying.

'No. We are too busy. I'll just have to send Rosina to collect the olives you forgot. If you had left earlier, none of this would have happened.'

'I'm sorry. I told you I didn't forget; I just wasn't able to go to the farm. My bicycle has a flat. If I'd got the olives from Uncle Luigi I would have been even later.' The woman's voice registered in Nic's mind. It sounded like the young woman who'd stepped in front of his car. *Brother? Papa?* She certainly hadn't looked like someone who belonged to an establishment as classy as this. Her soft apologetic tones were very different from the voice of the woman who'd called him an *idiota* only a few minutes ago. He shrugged and turned his attention back to the menu but the voices continued.

'I knew I should have asked Louisa. At least I have one

sister I can rely on.'

A large bear of a man with a white apron over his shirt hurried down the stairs and shot Nic an embarrassed smile before he too disappeared behind the curtain. His booming voice carried across the small space to Nic's table, louder than both the others. 'Gabriel, do not speak to your sister like that. Your voice is carrying all the way upstairs.'

'But Papa, she is late again—'

'Enough, you will leave her alone. Now go upstairs and see to the customers.'

Papa is obviously the boss. Nic looked away as the young man shoved the curtain aside and hurried up the steps. Family businesses—the same everywhere. Another reason why Nic knew he'd be much happier doing his own thing. Although the frequency of the arguments between he and Antonio had decreased ever since Nic had taken over looking after the quarries and the export contracts, Antonio had focused on the financial side of the business. Their father had insisted on them rotating through the company roles before he'd retired and Nic loved working with the marble, seeing it quarried and touching the beautiful final product before it was shipped all over the world. He was happy to stay in the business, so long as it was the creative side, but he knew he would be heading back to Florence soon. They had so many new contracts coming up Nic couldn't afford to indulge himself by being at the quarry for much longer. His mother's artistic genes might be the dominant ones, but his business degree ensured that he could run the business as his father had before Mamma died.

'Gia.' The man who was obviously their father spoke kindly. Nic unashamedly leaned across to listen. Maybe it was rude to eavesdrop but he wanted to be certain the young woman was all right.

'I'm sorry, *bella*. Gabriel is stressed because we are so busy tonight. Calm yourself, and don't let your brother upset you. We cannot have that, can we, *bella?* I will take the front section of downstairs and you will only have a small section to look after tonight. Please don't be upset.'

'Thank you, Papa.' The subdued and meek voice no longer sounded like the woman who Nic had met up the road. He frowned.

Perhaps I'm wrong.

The curtain opened and the man walked slowly over to his table. Nic caught a glimpse of a woman running up the stairs but the large man blocked most of the view and he couldn't see if it was his gypsy from the road.

'*Buonasera*. Welcome to *Giannino's*.' The man filled Nic's water glass from the bottle he'd carried over. 'I am Mauro.' He put the water bottle on the table in front of Nic and held his hands out widely. His handlebar moustache bobbed as he moved. 'We are very pleased to welcome you here tonight.' He lowered his head. 'I am very sorry you had to hear that small altercation. My daughter is a little upset tonight.'

'No problem. I hope she is okay?' Nic leaned back and looked around when Mauro nodded. 'You are doing a fine trade tonight.'

'*Pfft.*' Mauro waved one hand dismissively. 'It is like this every night. We love our guests. Are you travelling through?'

'No, I am staying at the *Casa Marmo* for a while.'

'Ah, the Baldini villa. Good to see it being rented out finally. That family has poured an obscene amount of money into renovating a place they never visit. And you know what? They did not employ one local tradesman. We are not good enough for the Baldinis. They think they bring the best from the city!'

After Mauro's disparaging comment, Nic wasn't about to tell him he was a Baldini and that he'd directed the renovations himself.

'Then hopefully we will see you again.' Mauro looked over Nic's shoulder. 'Ah, *bella,* there you are. Here is my beautiful daughter who will look after you, tonight. Gia will take your order and ensure that you wish to dine with us again during your stay.' Nic smothered a smile as Mauro clapped his hands together and introduced his daughter with a flourish as he beamed down at her. 'Have a good evening, *signore*.'

The young woman stepped around the bottom of the stairs and her gaze settled on Nic. It *was* his little gypsy from the incident on the roadside. The ugly black glasses still graced her face but her hair was now loose and framed her face in a wave of rich, black curls. The dark smear was gone from her face; her brother's word was obviously law, despite her Papa running interference for her. Huge dark eyes widened behind the spectacles as she recognised Nic. Her tanned skin darkened as a blush stained her cheeks. Gia pulled an order pad from the front pocket of the bright red apron that now covered her crumpled clothes. She nodded at Nic as her father moved away to the group at the next table.

'Have you had a chance to look at the menu yet, *signore*? Or perhaps you would prefer to avail yourself of our *primo* food table.' Her voice was soft and gentle, but the lilting Tuscan accent still held the husky undertone he'd heard before. This meek waitress was nothing like the little firebrand who had called him an idiot and poked him in the chest. This shy Gia didn't even meet his eyes as she gestured to the large table laden with tiers of food beneath the window.

So, she's going to pretend nothing happened.

Nic settled back in his chair and watched her. The change in her demeanour was fascinating. He would have teased her, perhaps made some joke about their last encounter. But having overheard her brother's heavy-handed rant, he would not add to her stress. 'No, I haven't had a chance to look at the menu yet. Perhaps you could recommend something?' A frisson of interest rippled through him as a quick smile tipped one corner of her mouth, and then disappeared just as quickly. A very pretty mouth, now that he had time to look at her. She knew very well who he was, but it looked like she was too shy—or embarrassed— to mention their earlier meeting.

Before she could tell him about the local delicacies, Nic's phone buzzed in his pocket. 'Excuse me for a moment, Gia.' He pulled it out and glanced at the screen.

Antonio. He had told him he was not to be contacted. *Unless there was a dire emergency.*

Chapter Four

Gia waited while the man from the sports car took his call. Trying not to be rude, or even listen to what he was saying, she waited, allowing the tone of his deep voice to wash over her. It was a voice she could almost transfer to canvas—sexy, full of hidden meaning and dark shadows, and it sent a shiver running down her back. She should have guessed that he was heading to *Giannino's*; most tourists headed their way for dinner at this time of year. It was the first restaurant on the edge of the village, and they were full every night during summer. If he'd been going any faster, she would probably be roadkill right now. But it really hadn't been his fault.

She'd been in such a bad mood she'd not been paying any attention to the traffic. Not that there was usually much traffic coming into the village on the way past her cottage. Most of the patrons of the restaurant came from the accommodation in the village and from the hotels on the north side. She wondered if he was staying locally or if he had just chanced upon the village.

There were only private villas further up her road. He was a very good-looking man and she pushed away the little tingle of attraction that rippled through her. His perfect grooming contrasted with her crumpled uniform and she smoothed her hand down her apron as she waited for him to finish his call.

Gia stepped back and looked through the window to the courtyard, trying not to listen to his conversation. Spring had been late arriving this year but now the courtyard was finally alive with vibrant summer colour. The honeysuckle covering the brick walls that closed in three sides was covered in fat yellow buds and the geraniums along the edge of the wall were a riot of red. It was one of the few things she enjoyed as she worked at the restaurant—the nights when she could look after the customers seated outside. Then, the work was much more pleasant. But the light rain tonight meant that all patrons were inside and the restaurant was packed to capacity. But hopefully, the tips would be good tonight. The more she earned, the sooner she could move to Florence.

'No.' The man's voice was terse and drew her attention back inside. 'Look, Antonio, I told you, I do *not* want to be interrupted while I'm down here.'

Gia studied him, partly embarrassed, partly impressed by the way he so bluntly expressed himself. The timbre of his voice was rich and deep as he made his point, and anger drew his brows together over his sharp eyes, and tightened his full lips.

'No, no and no. Do you get that?'

If they didn't, they weren't listening very well. Mr Perfectly Groomed Black Shirt was very clear in what he was saying. Gia continued to watch as she waited for him to finish his conversation, wishing she had the inner strength to say what *she* wanted in those confident tones. She caught her lip between her teeth as she recalled the way she'd called him an *idiota*.

Oh dear, that had been rude of her. And she had to wonder if perhaps her foul mood had triggered his.

Broad shoulders strained his shirt. He raked a hand through his jet-black hair and shifted in his seat. Sharply-defined cheekbones sat high in a tanned face. His bottom lip was full even though both lips were now pursed into a dissatisfied expression.

Movie star looks. A quiver of something ran through Gia's nerve endings and settled low in her belly. Heat ran up into her cheeks for the second time tonight. Okay, so he'd caught her checking him out. She had an eye for beauty and she'd already noted he was certainly a fine-looking man.

Oh, to paint him.

Gia swallowed when she realised he'd finished his call and was staring at her. She quickly put her head down and focused on her order pad, ignoring the gaze that she knew stayed on her face. She could *feel* him looking at her, and the warmth in her cheeks travelled through her body.

'Sorry about that. You were about to tell me what you would recommend?' His deep voice washed over her.

The heat flared again as he spoke. She was tempted to use the order pad to fan her face, but that would only draw his attention to her embarrassment. She peeked over the top of the order pad, though it certainly wasn't big enough to hide behind. Amused cerulean-blue eyes fanned by the longest eyelashes she had ever seen stared at her as he waited for her to answer.

'*Signore.*' She put the order pad down on the table and dug deep for courage. 'First, I think an apology is in order.'

'Apology? For what?' Those blue eyes were suddenly full of mirth. Better than the look that had been on his face when he'd been on his phone

'For calling you an *idiota*.' She rushed on and moved closer to him, brushing the stray strands of hair that fell across her face, impeding her vision as she leaned forward. 'It was entirely my fault and I wasn't watching where I was going. I'm so very, very sorry I was rude to you. I should not have been.'

'Apology accepted. Let's forget we have already met. Perhaps we can begin again?' He stood and held out his hand and Gia looked at him as she put her hand in his. For a moment, she thought he was going to kiss her fingers, and her heart sped up a notch, but he turned it over and examined her paint-stained fingers.

'I am Nic . . . and you are Gia.' He grinned at her and her heart gave another funny little blip; he truly was one of the sexiest men she had ever seen. The voice, the eyes, the dimple . . . the whole damned package.

She pulled her hand from his and slipped it into the pocket of her apron, conscious of her paint-stained fingers. *Probably not very hygienic in a restaurant.* It was a wonder Gabriel hadn't noticed them. 'I shall not bother you any longer. Are you ready to order?'

'Bother me?' He smiled at her. 'How would you be bothering me?'

His deep voice sent her nerve endings running wild—not to mention the sexy bedroom eyes that were holding hers. Oh dear, she was well and truly out of her element here.

Gia held up her order pad and tried to regain a measure of calm. 'What would you like for dinner, sir?'

Chapter Five

A strange, yet familiar, fragrance washed over Nic when Gia pulled her hand from his. Her fingers were stained with paint and the not-very-intoxicating perfume of turpentine came from her skin. That explained the streak on her face earlier. Ignoring her request for his order, he narrowed his eyes as interest quickened in him. 'You are an artist?'

Gia lifted her head and returned his gaze coolly before inclining her head in a simple nod. Her pen was poised above the order pad. 'I would recommend the *ribollita,* to begin with. It is made from vegetables grown locally in the village. The herbs come from the garden in our courtyard.'

Nic got the impression that she didn't want to answer his questions, so she had launched into her waitress spiel with her standard description of the menu. Unless perhaps, she was very shy. She obviously didn't want to engage in any personal conversation. He always found it difficult to turn away from anyone who needed encouragement. His mother had told him it was his Cancerian nature. He thought it was a load of rubbish but Antonio delighted in ribbing him about their mother's insistence that Nic had been entitled to more teenage angst than he was, because of Nic's astrological chart.

Don't know about Venus rising in Mercury, you're just a moody bastard. Nic had been tempted to punch his brother's lights out after that comment.

Nah, I'm just a sucker for anyone needy. And that's why he was so interested in this little waitress who waited for his order. Nic pushed the need to one side and focused on the menu before he looked up at Gia with a smile.

'Then the *ribollita* it is.' He put the menu down as she waited for him to continue. 'I'll look at the rest after I have my *primo* course.'

'Certainly, sir.' Gia scribbled on the order pad. 'Shall I bring you a selection or would you prefer to serve yourself?'

'I shall serve myself.' Nic reached up and caught her hand. 'And please? Call me, Nic.'

'Certainly, Nic.' Gia nodded again before she removed her hand from his and turned away, walking across to the other side of the restaurant.

She may have brushed her hair and washed the paint from her face, but Nic wondered if she knew about the small tear in the back of her white shirt. Her olive-tanned skin was exposed in a narrow slit beneath her shoulder, and there was a glimpse of pale pink lace. Much more feminine and softer than he'd expect from the prickly woman who'd refused his assistance, and much sexier than the black and white waitress uniform she wore over it. He shook his head, settled back, and picked up the glass of water as he observed the restaurant around him. A series of small paintings covered the wall behind the buffet and the colourful landscapes caught his eye. They were different from the generic prints that were sold by the hawkers in the squares around Florence. The crowd around the *primo* table had cleared and Nic picked up his empty plate and walked across. Everything from antipasto to pizza was on offer on the food-laden table.

Nic stood to the side of the table and narrowed his eyes, ignoring the food in front of him and looked at the wall. The small landscapes were . . . exceptional. He hadn't seen anything so fresh for a long time.

If ever. To stay in touch with his art, he attended as many exhibitions as he could. What stood out in each of the paintings in front of him was the minute detail of the flowers, the scarlet heads bobbing in a breeze he could almost feel. The artist had captured the distinctive bluish light of the Tuscan hills to perfection. The silence of the hills replaced the noise of the restaurant around him until a deep voice interrupted his intense observation.

'Gia likes to dabble in her spare time.' Mauro stood beside him with a frown on his face. 'We try hard to ask her to work with her sister in her shop in the village in the daytime, but—' the burly man threw his hands in the air in frustration—

'she will not listen to her Papa. I know she will be disappointed. She should be thinking about settling down, raising a family, and not chasing her foolish dreams.'

Nic widened his eyes. 'These are Gia's?'

Mauro sighed and nodded. 'Yes, she wanders the fields and then paints what is in her head. She is very stubborn and we try to protect her from disappointment. It is not a life for her.'

'Are they for sale?' Nic pointed to the four paintings on the wall in front of them. Her father almost made her sound simple, but the Gia he had encountered certainly didn't meet that description.

Mauro raised his shoulders. 'We have never thought of that. I would have to ask Gia.' He turned to Nic with a frown. 'You really think someone would pay money for these little paintings?'

'I would like to buy them all.' Nic stared at the man, shocked that he couldn't see the talent, the passion, that screamed out at him from each of the landscapes.

Protect her from disappointment? Not a life for her? Nic hadn't seen talent like this in a long time, not from any of his past protégées or even in exhibitions in Rome or New York.

Frustration clawed at his throat. *What I would give to be able to capture a scene like this with the stroke of my brush.* But all the money in the world couldn't buy talent like that on the wall in front of them. It made him all the more determined to put his time here to good use. He sympathised with Gia. They both had families who saw their art as a waste of time.

'I will ask Gia.' Mauro pointed back to Nic's table. 'Your soup is waiting.'

'Thank you . . . and no matter. I will ask her myself.' Nic smiled at Mauro. 'I still must complete my order.'

Mauro frowned and shook his head. 'I am afraid you won't be able to ask her. My daughter has gone home. She was not . . . well.'

'Is she okay?' Hoping it was not delayed shock that he had caused, Nic frowned. 'Where does she live?' He immediately regretted asking when Gia's father pulled himself up and stared at him. For a moment, he'd forgotten he was in rural Tuscany and not sophisticated Florence.

'My daughter does not live at home. It would not be right to give her address to a stranger.'

'Does she have a studio where she works where I could see her work when she is feeling better? Does she exhibit anywhere?'

'No, of course, she doesn't.' Mauro frowned and shook his head. 'But I will ask her if she is interested in selling her little paintings.'

For Christ's sake. Her little paintings. Nic couldn't

believe the dismissive tone in her father's voice.

Empathy filled him for the shy, young woman he had met so briefly. No wonder he had sensed that passion in her if she was capable of producing amazing work like this. Her father's disinterest made him doubt that he would even mention his interest to his daughter. Nic wondered if anyone else had asked about her work before and the message hadn't been passed on to her. No wonder she looked as though she had no confidence in herself, if this was the way her family treated her.

'Perhaps you could call back tomorrow. I will ask her for you.' His tone was not very enthusiastic, and Nic got the impression that Mauro was less than impressed with his interest in his daughter . . . or her paintings.

One or the other.

'Thank you.' Nic nodded and headed back to the table. He quickly finished his bowl of soup, declining the wine list when Gabriel reappeared and held it out to him

'No wine, thank you.' Nic's appetite had gone and had been replaced by a desire to go back to the villa and paint. Creativity surged through him and his fingers tingled with the urge to hold a brush. He had been inspired by Gia's landscapes. If she was willing to sell them, he had the perfect spot for them above his desk back in Carrara. He could take some of the countryside back with him to remind him of his promise to his mother.

Odd thing was, when he thought about leaving, it was the image of Gia, not the countryside, that filled his mind . . . and he didn't want to go.

***

Gia walked slowly up the hill. Papa's words as she departed rattled around in her head with every step she took.

'Are you ill? Have you been getting enough sleep? Have you been eating well?'

Yada, yada, yada. Same old story. No, she was not ill. No, she was not in need of rest or food. What she needed was to escape! When she had gone to the kitchen with Nic's order, Gabriel's snide comment about the tear in the back of her shirt had been the last straw. Tears had threatened; not because she was upset by her brother's words—she'd been putting up with them since they had been small children—but because of the frustration with the events of the night. She'd sought her father out and told him she wasn't feeling well and was going home . . . now.

And she should have known better than that, too. Of course, Papa had followed her as she'd collected her bag from the small room at the back of the kitchen.

He fussed around Gia like a mother hen and she bit back the impatient words that hovered on her lips. Instead of going home to her cottage, he'd wanted her to go home to be looked after by Mamma.

For goodness' sake, I'm not a sickly child anymore. The words had stayed in her mind and she'd thanked him politely. 'I will be fine at my place, Papa. It is only a headache.' Gia had gained a measure of smug satisfaction at her brother's frown on the way out. Let Gabriel take over her tables. He loved the work here. He could do it all. She barely refrained from poking her tongue out at him as she stepped into the courtyard.

The bottom line was: she just didn't want to be here. Not at the restaurant, not in Castellina. The studio at the back of her little cottage was the only thing that fulfilled her. *When I can paint, and put my feelings onto the canvas.* That's what brought life to her soul. Not serving food to an endless procession of tourists, night after night, and being wrapped in cotton wool by her well-meaning father.

What Gia really craved was to paint in a studio in Florence—studying her craft, going to college and mixing with like-minded people. Learning new techniques, not relying on old art books from the village library, and traipsing around galleries on the very rare occasions when she got to Florence.

Oh, to be able to spend my days painting. But Gia knew that wouldn't come without working in the family restaurant for the next couple of years in order to save enough money to be able to support herself in the city. Patience was not her strongest suit. The frustration of not having control of her future drove Gia crazy.

The look on her father's face a few months ago when she'd asked him to lend her enough money to move to Florence had been almost comical. You would have thought that she'd asked if she could sell herself into white slavery! He'd come up with many excuses why he couldn't lend her enough to set up her base in the city but as a sweetener for his refusal, he'd begrudgingly agreed to put some of her paintings up in the restaurant. Though he'd shown little interest in them, they were up.

It was just so unfair.

Papa had bought the leather bag shop for Louisa, her older sister, in the *Via della Volte,* the ancient tunnel in the medieval walls that now formed the shopping and restaurant area of Castellina. Gabriel had been sent away to Rome to do his hospitality training and all Gia had asked for was enough money to move to Florence.

But Gia had determination and passion in bucket loads. Her family just didn't know that. She had made a promise to herself that she would succeed. Louisa could sell her bags, Gabriel could run the finest restaurant in the land, and she, the baby of the family, would show the lot of them. *She* would be a famous artist.

I'm good enough. If only she could move to Florence where she'd prove it to her family.

Gia kicked the stones along the side of the road as she walked slowly up the hill, scuffing her shoes in the process. The full moon was high and the sky was a brilliant tapestry of millions of diamond stars. The slight breeze had cleared the clouds away and brought with it the fragrance of lavender from the fields. Lost in a world of her own, Gia thought of the colours she would mix when she got home. No matter how poor the light, she could still get some outlines onto her canvas now and then fill in the correct depth of colour tomorrow morning when the sun was bright and pouring through the large window at the back of her studio.

Even though she was lost in her thoughts, this time she heard the car coming up the hill behind her when the driver changed gear. She stepped to the side as anticipation rushed through her, even as she wondered why she was hoping it was Nic from the restaurant. It couldn't be; he would barely have finished his first course by now and, knowing Papa, he would have taken over her tables and he would be telling Nic the same funny anecdotes about the village he told the customers each night. Papa was a good man, even though he didn't realise his baby daughter was now a grown woman.

Gia sighed as she waited for the car to pass her. Maybe she should just move to Florence and look for a job there. She could earn more money and save more quickly. But the problem was that she had no qualifications except as a waitress. She had only worked in the family business. No way would Gabriel and Papa give her the references she would need to find a job in a restaurant in the city.

The car slowed and pulled to a stop behind her. Gia turned slowly and her eyes widened. The moonlight glinted off the chrome of the fancy sports car.

'Can I offer you a ride?' The deep tones of the already familiar voice reached her as Nic climbed out of the car.

'I'm fine, thank you. I'm almost home.' She could remain calm now. *Sophisticated and calm.* Despite the scuffs on her shoes and the stain on her skirt. Despite her earlier rudeness.

'I'm pleased I caught up with you. I wanted to talk to you.'

She pushed her glasses higher on her nose as he walked around the front of the car to join her. Funnily enough, they were at the spot where they'd met earlier.

'Why would you want to do that? Wasn't your soup to your taste?' She didn't intend to be smart-mouthed but the words came out sounding rude. But he didn't appear fazed by it. A glimmer of a smile played about his lips.

'The soup was very good. Thank you for suggesting it,' he said politely.

'So? What else could you possibly want to talk to me about?' Gia frowned. It wouldn't be her looks that had attracted him.

'I was worried you were unwell because of the near miss before.'

'Pfft.' She waved her hand dismissively. 'That was nothing.'

He stared at her intently and Gia lifted her chin and returned his look. Measured him up, appreciating him with her eye for beauty. Once again, she was hit with the realisation of what a good-looking man he was. No—if a man could be called beautiful, he was that. Even in the moonlight, she could see his large dark eyes, long eyelashes, high cheekbones and sexy, full lips. His voice sent a jolt rippling through her nerve endings. Gia dropped her eyes to travel down to his broad shoulders, past his narrow hips, lingering on long legs that she knew would be muscular beneath those snug-fitting black jeans. Not that she had much experience at looking at men's legs; most of her knowledge of the structure of a man's body had come from her observation of Michelangelo's statue of David during her visits to the *Galleria dell' Accademia* in Florence. Her only other observation had been her long-time boyfriend in her late teens.

But Stefano had been too keen on the marriage and baby route. He was now settled in the next village, happily married to a local girl and with a couple of children already.

Much to her parent's disappointment. And Stefano's legs did not compare to either David's or this man's. She shivered. Stefano had been a close call. Gia looked up at Nic's face, trying to ignore the pounding of her heart. Why had her thoughts taken her in that direction?

Nic's lips were curved in a grin, telling her he was well used to being admired. And that he didn't mind at all.

Dio, this man did . . . things to her. She focused on the cute dimple in his chin and stood straight. Even though she was tall, she still had to tip her head back to see his face.

'Good, I am pleased you are okay.'

Okay? No way. Butterflies were fluttering through her stomach. *Forget it.* Nic's fine clothes, his fancy car, his movie actor good looks . . . this man was way out of her league. He would never be remotely interested in her. A waitress from a little village like Castellina? When he drove a car that was worth more than she would earn in ten years.

'Gia?'

She shook her head. 'Yes?' What was he going to ask her? His dark gaze was intent and his expression was so serious.

'I wanted to talk to ask you about your paintings.'

'*My* paintings?' That was the last thing she expected him to say.

'If you're the artist who created those landscapes back in the restaurant. Unless your father was joking?'

'Of course he wasn't joking. And yes, they are mine, but I am surprised he showed them to you.' Gia tried to keep the bitterness from her voice. After all, why would this man be remotely interested in her or her paintings? She couldn't really understand why he had stopped to ask about her work.

'So, they are yours?'

'I just said they were.' Gia stared at him.

'Can I buy them?'

Gia screwed her face into a confused frown. 'Why?'

'Because they are very good.' He wasn't smiling now. When Gia realised he was serious, a tendril of excitement unfurled in her chest.

'Um . . . er . . . you've—'

'Do you have any more?' Nic reached out and took her arm. The expression on his face was akin to yearning. Gia's heart gave one huge leap.

'Any more what?'

'Landscapes. Or other paintings?'

Gia wanted nothing more than to grab his hand and drag him up the road into her cottage, turn the lights on, and show him the dozens of canvases that graced the walls of her studio. There *were* more small pictures like those in the restaurant, but she had many more full-sized canvases of her landscapes.

But of course, she didn't take his hand. Too many years of having her work criticised and dismissed as unimportant by her family ran deep in her veins and she imagined she would only be disappointed one more time.

'Look, I really have to get home.' She turned away from him, but he still held her arm gently, and then curiosity got the better of her. Turning back to face him, she narrowed her eyes and tried to keep her voice free of uncertainty. 'What do you know about art? Why would you think my paintings are good?'

Cerulean eyes held hers. 'Because I dabble in art, and I have never been so touched as I was by the movement in your landscapes.'

Chapter Six

Nic held Gia's arm lightly; the moonlight highlighted her wide eyes and he was scared she would scamper away like the frightened rabbit she reminded him of. No wonder she seemed to lack assurance in herself. He'd seen the way her father had dismissed her work. A talent like hers deserved to be recognised. No, more than recognised; it *must* be exhibited. It should be shared with the world. It was a crime for such a talent to be hidden away in a small village like Castellina.

Already, his thoughts surged ahead. He was planning his tactics, ready to persuade Gia to listen to him. As much as he hated it, he'd switched into business mode. Lately, that came more with more frequency than his creative muse. Odder still, he liked the surge of excitement that accompanied it. To present an artist, discovered by him . . . that is if the rest of her work was to his standard.

He sought the right words to convince her—without scaring her off, and without sounding too pushy. He would sponsor her. He would organise an exhibition. That was if she had enough work completed. Thinking quickly, Nic had a plan formulated in his head, before he spoke his thoughts aloud. He'd plan every last detail and could introduce her to the art world he loved. She didn't need to know who he was; he wasn't going to leave himself open again. Gia seemed sincere but he'd fallen for that ruse before. He would take control and it would be good for her. Without someone supporting her, she could spend her life painting in this rustic village, undiscovered and unknown. Anticipation flooded through Nic; it would be a great feeling to help her achieve success and she would never have to know it was the Baldini benevolent fund that gave her a start in the art world. Because he had no doubt she had the talent. But did she have the staying power to make it in the art world?

None of his previous protégés had as much talent as he'd seen in those four small landscapes. And not one of them had the dedication to develop the talent they did have . . . not when the money flow had stopped.

Go carefully. Don't get too excited.

Nic let go of Gia's arm and stepped back to give her some space. He looked past her down to the village. The tall tower of the Fortress of Castellina was lit up by a spotlight providing a beacon to the centre square of the village. A soft blue light played on the high tower.

Gia stepped back and folded her arms. Despite the shadows, Nic could see the frown that wrinkled her forehead again, and then her spectacles slipped down her nose. She pushed them up impatiently with a paint-stained finger. 'I knew there was something famous about you. You looked familiar to me.'

'No, I'm not famous. Certainly not a famous artist.' Nic's laugh was slightly bitter as he shook his head.

I wish.

'I have an eye for art, Gia. And you are exceptionally talented.'

'Really? Do you really think that?' The uncertainty in her voice almost broke his heart. Her family had done a real number on her confidence.

'And what do you mean, you dabble?' She tipped her head to the side and stared at him curiously as though dabbling and art did not belong in the same sentence

'I mean I love to paint, but I don't get much time for it.' Nic's laugh was slightly bitter as he shook his head. If only he could live in this countryside and paint all day, every day. 'I'm here on holidays and I will paint while I'm here. Like many tourists who come to visit this region.' He stepped to the car and opened the passenger door. 'Look, why don't you come with me, and we can go back down into the village for a drink? I'd love to hear more about your techniques.'

'Uh-uh.' Gia shook her head and turned around, pointing to her stained clothes. 'I'm in no state to go anywhere.'

'So how about I drive you home and you can get

changed?' Nic stood back as she observed him and he knew he was being summed up.

'Where are you staying?' she finally said.

'I am staying at a place a few miles along the road.'

'Where?' She was persistent and although he should say the Baldini villa—Mauro's reaction had been enough for one night—he admired her caution.

'One of the private villas. So, what do you say? Will you trust me enough to go for a drink in the village?'

Gia stood back and Nic watched as one scarlet-tipped finger tapped her bottom lip. He smiled; he was more used to escorting women who had long fingernails scarlet from expensive manicures, not because they'd dipped their fingers into paint.

'Please? I'd really like to show you how sorry I am for causing you that fright on your bike. I was going to look for you tomorrow in the village, but finding you tonight was meant to be.' He didn't want to be too pushy, so he waited while she looked at him.

'Okay, but how about some *gelato* instead of a drink? I haven't eaten yet today. I've been too busy.'

'How about dinner, then?'

Gia laughed and the sound was attractive. 'I thought you had dinner already? Vegetable soup?' Her face broke into a grin and the interest that had been stirring in Nic's chest firmed into something more tangible. Her lips were softly parted and even as he chuckled, he appreciated the sweet cupid shape of her top lip. In all her glorious disarray, she was quite lovely. If you took away the ghastly spectacles and tamed the wild mane of hair that was standing in a messy cloud around her head, she might be quite presentable. The smile softened her serious face, and Nic was pleasantly surprised by the change in her attitude.

'Okay, ice-cream does it for me. Where do we go?'

Gia walked across the car and opened the passenger door. 'If you are happy to take me home first, and wait for me while I get changed, I'll take you to the best *gelataria* in all of Italy.'

'All of Italy? That's a big call.' Nic followed her and held the car door open.

She grinned up at him as she slid into the low-slung car. 'Everywhere I've been, anyway.'

And that was probably not many places. His impression of the village—and her family—was that this was where life was lived. Not like the jet-setting life of his family. Skiing in the Swiss Alps, swimming on the French Riviera. That was why the Baldinis hadn't used the Tuscan villa enough to make the locals happy. They had houses all around Europe. But it was not the time to share that; he didn't want to frighten her off. He *had* to see more of her work.

He'd made progress, and now that Gia had agreed to come with him, he'd have a chance to see it. He vaulted over the side of the car and slipped into the driver's seat.

Gia shook her head and smiled at him as he started the car. 'I'm not that easily impressed, you know. I've got a big brother. Macho stuff doesn't work for me.'

The Roadster purred along the road, and the silence was companionable while he waited for directions to her cottage.

'I met your brother tonight.' He flicked a glance over to her. She was leaning back, letting the breeze rush over her face and her hair was in even wilder disarray. Untamed. His fingers tingled as he thought of running his hands through that wild mass of curls. Had he thought her hair a messy cloud? The lush curls were gorgeous.

'Lucky you.' A soft chuckle escaped her lips. 'Poor Gabriel, he doesn't know when to stop. Usually, I don't let him bother me, but tonight—'

Nic was aware of her studying his profile as he focused on driving up the hilly road.

'Tonight?' he prompted when she didn't continue.

Gia pointed to an opening just beyond a stand of trees, and he slowed the car and turned in to park beside a low wooden gate. Before she could open the car door, he stepped over the low door on his side and walked around to open hers. He held his hand out to help her up from the passenger seat and satisfaction ran through him as she dropped her gaze. She was reticent, but the sparks were smouldering beneath the surface. Her fingers lingered in his for a few seconds after she climbed out.

'I'll be quick.' She ventured a shy smile as she pulled her hand from his and turned to the gate.

As he waited by the car, Nic appreciated the view of her long, shapely legs as she hurried across to the stone cottage. He didn't want to scare her off, even though she did appear more comfortable with him. He was anxious to see the rest of her paintings, and he was keen to get to know her on a different level, but he would bide his time. Many of the business deals he'd pulled off in the last year had called on his patience and often involved playing a cat-and-mouse game. So, he wasn't going to appear overeager to Gia. He had a feeling she'd run like the startled rabbit he'd compared her to before.

First priority. Win her trust.

Seeing her work would come a close second. Nic leaned back against the car and looked around. The moonlight was bright enough to see the buildings beyond the gate Gia had closed behind her. An old stone farmhouse with a couple of small outbuildings sat on the side of the hill, with a magnificent view out over the valley and the village below. Everywhere he looked, there was a landscape waiting to be painted.

A few minutes later, when the door closed behind Gia, an outside light came on, bathing the building in bright light. The faded pink stone had the aged look of an original Tuscan farmhouse, and the weathered shutters hung crookedly from some of the small windows. Other windows were missing their shutters. The only thing that was well-maintained was the yard. From the other side of the gate to the door that Gia had disappeared through, the lawn was dark and lush but clipped neatly along the edges.

A paved area next to the small building was filled with weathered, half wine casks and flowers spilled over their sides. Small circular gardens were planted around the bases of the tall spreading trees that dotted the lawn. It would make a wonderful subject for a still-life piece. Despite his mind being focused on the landscapes he had seen tonight, Nic's fingers tingled with the need to hold a paintbrush and replicate what was in front of him. The moonlight made the scene even more enticing. What would make it perfect would be Gia as the focus of the painting, her classically beautiful face turned up to the moon. Nic jerked his thoughts back to reality and stifled a laugh.

The moon.

His mother would have been most impressed. Neither he nor his brother had held regard for her obsession with the star signs, but she'd made sure he knew all about the Cancerian behaviours she believed would guide his life. A pang of sadness ran through him. He thought he'd grieved long and hard enough, but memories of his mother had filled his thoughts since he'd arrived.

Nic shook off his feeling as the door closed. He watched Gia walk slowly across the lawn to him.

Or at least he thought it was Gia. The woman who opened the gate looked very different from the young waitress who'd left him waiting in the sports car. Nic's breath caught and he managed to ask, 'All set?' before he dragged in a deep breath. The baggy clothes, the wild hair and the black spectacles were gone.

Gia looked at him from beneath her lashes as she closed the gate and slid into the passenger seat while he held the door open for her. 'I'm not sure this is such a good idea.' Her voice was hesitant. 'If Gabriel finds out I went out tonight after going home ill, I'll be out of a job.'

'But doesn't your father own the restaurant? Wouldn't your brother understand?' Nic had regained his breath and his voice was steady. *But not so the rest of him.* A tremble ran down his spine. Gia was more than attractive; she was beautiful.

'Gabriel is the manager. He wouldn't be happy. They were very busy tonight. I should've stayed.' Her voice was resigned.

'Do you like working there?' Nic fought the need to keep his eyes on Gia, so he focused on starting the car. Her delicate perfume—something fruity—drifted over to him.

Strawberries.

'No, I hate it.' She folded her arms across her chest and Nic tried to keep his eyes away from the soft shadow between the swell of her breasts. Despite her slender build, there was certainly nothing lacking beneath her low-neck fitted T-shirt.

'So why do you stay there?' Nic put the car into reverse and backed out onto the narrow road. He put his arm along the back of the seat as he looked back to the road, and his fingers accidentally brushed against Gia's skin. She'd pulled it up into some sort of topknot and it had left her neck bare. Nick ignored the urge to run his fingers down the slender curve.

'Sorry.' He put his hand back on the steering wheel and turned the car back towards the village.

'I have to pay my rent.' She gave a rueful shrug. 'Although it is not much, it's an old farmhouse and it's run down. I also have to buy my canvases and my paints.' Her reply was soft. 'And it makes my father happy—having me work there with the rest of the family.'

They didn't speak again until they'd passed the restaurant and taken the last hill down toward the village. Gia pointed to a building on the left side of the crossroad. 'Over there.'

Nic parked the car across the road from the brightly-lit *gelateria.* He'd intended to do the gentlemanly thing and open the door for Gia but she was out and waiting on the kerb before he could shut his door. Certainly not what he was used to. The women he usually took out expected to be pampered and looked after by their escorts. But then, they were usually with him at the theatre or a fancy restaurant, not an ice-cream shop in a little village in the Tuscan countryside. But he never took a date to his gallery visits. That was one place he always went alone. He didn't want to have to pander to someone else when he was absorbed in appreciating the latest exhibition. And it was an interest he kept private. Not even Antonio knew why Nic came to Tuscany. Only his father knew of his desire to paint. Antonio had been too young to notice when Nic had been in his teens.

Despite her hesitancy, there was an aura of confidence about Gia—Nic couldn't quite figure out the two different sides he was seeing, but he was going to enjoy finding out. He checked the car was secure and joined her at the edge of the curb and smiled. 'You must be hungry.'

She walked ahead of him as they crossed the road. She wore a short black skirt and her legs were bare, her feet in colourful sandals. Her T-shirt, moulding the curves he'd checked out in the car, was a dark scarlet. The curves that hadn't been apparent beneath the frumpy waitress uniform.

Nic was surprised again when Gia paused outside the shop and peered at the crowd inside. He frowned. She really was intimidated by her family. Maybe this idea of his wasn't such a good one? He could see complications arising if it was such a big deal just to go out and buy ice-cream.

And then Nic thought of those paintings he'd seen in the restaurant. It would be worth it.

Chapter Seven

Gia was already regretting ditching her spectacles. The problem was, she'd only been able to find one of her contact lenses amongst all the bottles and jars scattered around her studio. She was well aware of Nic standing beside her, even though he was only a fuzzy shape. The woodsy aftershave was enough of a dead giveaway as to how close he was to her, and the warmth tingling on her skin warned her that he was close enough for her to lean into him—if she wanted to.

And she did.

It had been a long time since she'd taken so much care with her appearance, and Gia was still trying to figure out why her common sense had fled. Maybe it was because being out with a sexy man—one who was interested in her art—was so different from her usual boring life. Maybe it was because Nic looked so . . . so perfect? He appealed to her artistic eye; that was all. The only stimulation Gia got in her predictable days was when she was painting. It was the only time she felt truly alive . . . and happy. There was nothing like the anticipation of looking at a blank canvas, imagining her thoughts and feelings and letting them fill the emptiness as bright splashes of colour. In a way, it filled the emptiness that she always carried inside.

She was alone in the midst of her vibrant family, but independence was important to her. None of her family understood the desire that drove her. They didn't even *know* it was inside her. All they saw were the boring clothes, the haphazard hair, and the huge spectacles she had to wear. No one ever took her *seriously*. Her family thought she needed protecting. God, she'd even overheard Papa tell Gabriel to go easy on his little "fragile flower" tonight. That was when Gia had had enough and decided to go home. Very much out of character—usually, she could ignore them, but Papa was trying to protect her from what?

Independence? Standing on my own two feet?

Now she turned to Nic and tried not to squint as she looked up at him. Half of his face was fuzzy and the other half was clear. Gia knew if she closed one eye, she'd be able to see him clearly but she didn't want to frighten him off by pulling faces.

She grinned. *Not until I've had my ice-cream, anyway.*

'What are you smiling about?' His warm breath brushed the nape of her neck as he leaned closer to speak to her. 'Not that I'm complaining.'

Gia was tall, but Nic was so much taller than she was that she had to put her head back to look at him.

'I'm happy.' She reached out and touched his arm.

Nic's deep voice rumbled through her. 'Then you're easy to please if all it takes is ice-cream.'

They strolled into the *gelataria* and Nic raised his eyebrows at the crowd of people in there. A small group of women with a mix of accents were deliberating over their choice. Gia recognised them from the restaurant the other night. They were authors from all over the world staying at the local hotel just a little way up from the restaurant. Gia had enjoyed serving them but she knew they didn't recognise her as the frumpy waitress from *Giannino's*. She leaned forward and spoke to one of the women.

'I can recommend the fig and ginger,' she said pointing to a tub of white ice-cream at the front of the display.

The woman turned to her with a smile; her accent was broad Australian. 'Nothing beats local knowledge. Come on, gals, hurry up and choose. We're holding up this sweet young couple.'

Couple? Gia stepped away from Nic. It was a long time since she'd been considered part of a couple. When she had broken up with Stefano, she had become used to her own company. But life could be lonely at times, and it *was* nice to have company tonight. The night had turned into something different and interesting and she had a good-looking man at her side.

Enjoy it while I can. Beats the hell out of clearing dirty dishes in the restaurant which is what she should be doing right now.

Heat rushed up Gia's neck when she caught Nic staring at her. She looked at the colourful display of ice-cream in the cabinet before turning back to him. She tipped her head to the side and tapped her chin with one finger. '*Hmm*. Let me guess. You'll choose the chocolate flavour?'

'Uh uh. Hate the stuff.' Nic's eyes crinkled as he smiled down at her.

Gia chuckled. 'How can anyone hate chocolate? My stash of chocolate means I don't have to cook.'

'You don't like to cook?'

Gia shook her head. 'Waste of time. Takes up time when I could be painting. What about you?'

Those sexy eyes crinkled again. 'I love to cook.'

She pondered what she knew of this man, his penchant for both the sophisticated and simple, as he ordered their gelato, hers, the recommended fig and ginger, while he opted for the strawberry. Nic insisted upon paying after she pulled money from her pocket. She appreciated his offer, but she was accustomed to taking care of herself.

'The invitation was mine,' he said. 'Allow me to pay. It's my pleasure.' He reached down and pulled a dark burgundy wallet from his jeans pocket.

Something in the way he said "pleasure" had her thinking things that sent a pleasant tingle buzzing through her. Covering her reaction, she nodded and whispered, '*Grazie.*' She stared at his wallet. It was almost her signature colour. 'What a beautiful colour that leather is. My sister has nothing so vibrant in her store. May I?' After he had pulled out a bill, she held out her fingers and smoothed the soft leather of his wallet. It was soft and pliant, and his initials were cut into the leather in a graceful swirl. She realised she didn't even know his full name. 'What does the *B* stand for, Nic?'

He handed the money over to the young girl behind the counter before he answered her. He took her arm and they stepped back to wait as she filled the order.

'Er . . . ah, my name . . . ah, you mean my last name? Yes. Battistoni. Nic Battistoni.' He looked away from her and reached for a wad of napkins from the dispenser on the counter. 'We might need these.' The ice-creams were handed over, and they stepped past the queue to the door that opened to the narrow street. They strolled back across the road with their ice-creams, laughing as their conversation turned into a guessing game.

'So, you hate chocolate. What's your choice? Coke or Pepsi?' she asked as she bit into the ice-cream.

'Coke,' Nic said and Gia pulled a face at him. 'Horror or

comedy?' he asked.

'Comedy, of course.' She laughed and led him over to a park bounded by a low stone fence at the edge of the hill. A vista of farmhouse lights spread across the valley in front of them.

He shook his head sadly at her answer. 'Batman or Superman?'

'Neither. Hate superheroes.'

'There's no hope for you then if you ever need rescuing.'

A tremor ran through Gia as she imagined being a damsel in distress rescued by Nic. She hated superhero movies, but she'd loved all those fairy stories when she was little. Just like he'd tugged her into his arms on the road this afternoon. Being swept into his arms again, her head tilting back as she stared into his eyes and her neck exposed to his lips as he lowered his head ... closer, closer. Her eyes closed as the flavour of the ice-cream burst on her tongue as sweet as she knew his kiss would be.

The laughter of the women walking up the road ahead of them broke into her thoughts. She ignored the heat that crept through her body as she imagined Nic's lips on hers. Fairy tales didn't happen in real life. You had to work to achieve what you wanted. And that was what she had to focus on.

The women's voices grew fainter, and the evening air was still as they both focused on eating the ice-cream before it melted. Eventually, the group disappeared over the crest of the hill and all was quiet.

Nic lifted his ice-cream to his mouth, and Gia resisted the urge to reach up and wipe away the spot of strawberry she could just see on his top lip after he lowered the cone. She wasn't going to touch him. Although she wanted to. Badly.

Gia pushed the thought aside and tipped her cone up and bit the bottom off.

Nic stared at her lips and that shivery feeling engulfed her again, but this time it travelled down to the warm juncture between her thighs.

'What are you doing?' His voice was full of laughter, but his eyes were fixed on her lips.

'It's the only way to experience *gelato*. Before the ice-cream melts and the cone goes all soggy.'

'Ah, an expert. Local knowledge.'

Gia swept her hand around in a huge arc. 'Do you know Castellina at all?'

'Not well. I've been here to paint for the last three years, but I haven't explored the valleys. It's the only real chance I get to paint.' Nic cleared his throat. 'During the summer.'

'So, you need a tourist guide? They are the Arbia, Elsa, and Pesa valleys and this is the crossroad on the road to Sienna. Gia laughed as he stared at her. 'I do sound like a guide, don't I? Valleys, *gelati* . . . anyone would think I loved the place.'

'Don't you?'

'I can't wait to escape if the truth be known.'

'From the restaurant?'

'The restaurant. My life here. My family. They don't get what drives me. They don't get what's *inside* me. I'm just Gia to them. The baby of the family who needs looking after. I can wear boring clothes, leave my hair untidy, and wear my ugly glasses, and they don't see *anything*.'

Nic reached out and touched her arm. His fingers were sticky with ice cream as they lingered on her wrist.

She swallowed and dropped her gaze. She wasn't used to this intensity of feeling when she was with another person. These were the feelings that filled her when she was painting. The warm glow, the keen anticipation, the wonder of how it would turn out.

She licked her top lip again and caught Nick's gaze as he followed the movement. He lifted his napkin.

'May I?' His head was close enough to her now, and she could focus on that dimple that was imprinted on her memory. She nodded and he dabbed at her lip. When he had finished, she rushed into conversation, filling the tense silence that had hovered between them after he had lowered the napkin.

'It's okay, I suppose. It's where I was born, and where I grew up. My family has been here for many generations.' Gia stared out over the quiet valley. 'But I want to *live* life. I want to paint more. I want to learn all there is to be learned out there in the world.'

She twisted her hands together. God, she was telling her life story to a stranger. But a stranger who made her come alive, just like when she was painting. In a way, she was pleased he had almost run into her this afternoon. It was the first *real* conversation with anyone apart from her family and customers she'd had in weeks.

'I sometimes think I could walk into the restaurant stark naked and they still wouldn't notice me.'

A blush warmed her cheeks when she saw the little smile play around Nic's lips. The air was humming with expectation, and she felt like she had entered fairy tale land. She knew exactly what he was thinking, and she held his gaze as he spoke, but his words surprised her.

'If it's any consolation, my father doesn't trust me to know what I want out of life, either.' As though he was reading her thoughts, Nic turned to her and pointed to the old stone bench at the back of the building at the side of the lookout. 'Come and sit down with me. You can tell me all about you. I know some.' He counted off on his fingers. 'Loves chocolate, doesn't cook, loves to paint, hates superheroes—'

Gia cut him off with a laugh. 'Me? It's a boring story.

There's not much to tell. In fact, I think you know it all already. Like I said, I've lived here all my life. I work in the family restaurant. My parents want me to get married and settle in the village and provide them with a tribe of grandchildren.' She brushed the crumbs from the cone off her lap before she lifted her head and held his gaze. 'I want to move to Florence and paint. A short and not very interesting life story.'

Nic moved closer to her on the seat and Gia finally gave in and closed one eye. With a bit of luck, he wouldn't notice. It *was* ice cream on his mouth. She pulled out the tissue she'd tucked between her breasts earlier and squinted as she reached over and dabbed the ice cream from his lip. He looked down at her and smiled, and she fought the little shiver that shimmied down her spine.

'Thanks. I love the way you concentrate so hard on everything you do. It must translate to your art. That must be how you get that magnificent detail into your work.'

Gia couldn't help letting out the laughter that bubbled in her chest. 'Do you want the truth?'

'The truth?'

'Yep. The vain truth. I didn't wear my glasses . . . so,'— her laugh tinkled away over the valley in front of them—'I am squinting so I can see your face more clearly.'

Nic's rumble of laughter touched Gia somewhere deep,

and the cold block of nothingness inside of her began to splinter. It had been a very long time since she had enjoyed someone's company so much and been her true self. She'd almost forgotten who she was. She'd become so used to pretending to be the person her family wanted; she'd almost morphed into the drab, meek waitress that they expected her to be. It was fun to laugh with somebody.

'I don't know *everything* about you.' Nic reached across and put his arm along the back of the bench. 'Look at you now. Clothes that fit you. No rips or tears in them.' He softened the words with a smile. 'So, tell me, do you always go to the restaurant looking like you did tonight?'

Gia leaned against his arm. His grin was a tiny bit blurry, but Gia could see the amusement on his face the closer she got. She shrugged. 'Most days. That is me. I'm not a very clean artist. And I am always running late.' She shrugged. 'So, you get me. You get the paint. My family is critical enough of me. I don't care what anyone else thinks.'

Nic's arm brushed her shoulder as he stretched out more comfortably. 'Well, I think you are a very beautiful woman, paint and all. When I almost ran into you as I came over the hill, I thought you might have been a gypsy. You reminded me of someone I met when I was a teenager.'

'No gypsies in the village anymore. They're all in the

cities now.' Gia rested her elbows on her knees and cupped her chin on her hands. 'Okay, let me try to explain. I guess dressing like that was my way to rebel.'

'Rebel?'

'Against my family. They see what they want to see. I'm the youngest of three and the other two are both hugely successful, and my parents are very proud of their achievements. Papa has always sheltered me. He thinks I'm the quiet one. He wants me to stay here.'

'So, you fulfill his expectations?'

'I guess it's like a reverse rebellion. They think I'm the quiet mouse in a vivacious family, so I decided it was easier to be what they wanted. Saves a lot of disagreements.' Gia sighed. 'As Papa tells me most days, staying in the village is for my own good. He honestly believes I wouldn't survive in a city only forty miles away. I guess he thinks if he tells me often enough, I'll give up the idea of moving away and accept what he says.'

'If you're really sure that's what you want, what your dream is'—Nic reached out and took her hand— 'I may be able to help.'

***

Nic was surprised at the genuine honesty that Gia was showing him, sharing her feelings with him. They had hit it off as soon as they had met—well, almost— if you discounted the incident on the road. Maybe it was the moonlight lighting up the valley in front of them. The whole scene was impossibly romantic. Gia intrigued him; there was absolutely no artifice about her. Discomfort rippled through him as he thought of the white lie he had told her. Well, it wasn't too bad a lie. Battistoni had been his mother's family name. He sent a little apology skywards.

Sorry, Mamma.

His mother would have been fascinated with Gia; she'd always loved uncovering the layers that a person hid behind, and Nic had a feeling that if he peeled away Gia's layers, she would find one very strong and determined woman. They had hit it off as soon as they had met—well, almost— if you discounted the incident on the road. Maybe it was the moonlight lighting up the valley in front of them; maybe it was that they were both relaxed. The whole scene was impossibly romantic. She intrigued him with her lack of artifice. Even though she was dressed in decent clothes now—he smothered a grin as he thought of the baggy clothes she deliberately hid behind in the restaurant—what he was looking at tonight was a real woman. Not the designer clothes, the dripping jewels and the heady perfumes he was used to. She was fresh and natural—sweet was the word he was trying to think of. The strawberry scent reinforced that freshness and her laughter when they'd discovered they were opposites in just about everything. He was having *fun*—for the first time in a long time.

He let go of Gia's hand and moved away. He wanted to see more of her work, and he knew he was going to have to tell her a little about himself, but he couldn't be Nic Baldini, millionaire businessman; he just wanted to be another artist who recognised talent. He'd heard what her father had thought of his family. Another ripple of guilt ran through Nic and he pushed it away. Maybe he should have employed some local tradesmen. He didn't want her to label him as a rich guy or simply a guy on the make. And he was wary, too. His wealth had been taken advantage of too many times before, and for that reason, he wasn't going to make the Baldini connection known. Not yet . . . he wanted—no, he needed to see more of her work. The landscapes he had seen had fired his interest.

'So, you want to move to Florence? You are sure that's where you want to be?'

'Yes, it is. But want do you mean "you can help"?' Gia frowned and her voice was tinged with something akin to suspicion.

Nic hurried on so she didn't think he was just some sleaze trying to sweet-talk her. He chose his words carefully. 'I would like to see some more of your work before I tell you what I am thinking.' He turned to face her and the moonlight outlined her profile as she looked down at the valley. 'If your other work is half as good as the landscapes . . . I need to see more. Will you show me others?'

'I'd like to know more about *you* before I agree to show you anything else.' Her eyes were narrowed and her voice careful, as though she was wondering why a chance-met stranger would want to help her. Sort of a reverse "come up and see my etchings".

'Tell me more about you. And not just what sort of movies you like.'

Maybe she did think he was trying to get her into bed—not that he'd mind that one little bit—but he wanted her to know that he was genuinely interested in what he'd seen of her work.

Nic leaned back on the seat and folded his arms. He wanted her to like him for himself and not for what he could do to help her. It had been a long time since he had had such a deep response to a woman, and he wanted to explore that feeling.

'I'm here on holidays. I am staying in a villa along the way, and I am going to paint.'

'Which villa?' Gia turned her head to the side and Nic swallowed. It wasn't a lie; it just wasn't the exact truth.

'The company I work for owns *Casa Marmo,* not far along the road from your cottage.'

It was very out of character for him to rush in and speak; it must have been the moonlight or the innocence of this sweet woman sitting beside him that had made him say that without thinking it through.

'You work for the Baldinis? The Carrara marble family?' she said.

Shit. Of course, she would know who owned the villa. He was not used to small village life. Just as well he'd never spent much time in Castellina. The caretaker had made sure the kitchen was stocked on the couple of visits he'd made before. He waited, wondering if she'd realise he was a Baldini. His family was well known, not that he paid any attention to such frivolous things. They weren't so famous to be hounded by paparazzi or plastered among society pages, but he'd been featured in multiple newspaper articles, especially for his contributions to the children's hospital in Florence. And his face had graced the covers of many business magazines.

'I don't sculpt, but it must be wonderful to work amid so much beautiful stone.' Gia's voice was full of awe, and guilt settled in Nic's stomach like . . . a stone. But at least she didn't have the same attitude as her father. And, even more of a blessing, there was no recognition in her expression and no censure in her voice.

'Er . . . yes. I work in the quarries.' It wasn't exactly a lie. It was close to the truth. He didn't have to say he ran the whole operation.

'I would so love to go there one day. My favourite man'—Gia grinned at him and Nic's heart did a funny little jump—'is made of Carrara marble.'

'Ah, the wonderful statue of David.' Nic swallowed, pushing away the need that coursed through his body as her strawberry fragrance enveloped him. At the same time, relief settled over him like a soft blanket. He could be himself here. The heat in his blood cooled a little when Gia moved the subject away from the Baldinis to his art.

'So, tell me about how you got into art. What do you paint?'

'Well, to be truthful,'—Nic swallowed, truthful was not the best choice of words—'you and I have very similar backgrounds. I've always painted—ever since I was a teenager, but my father has always dismissed it as a waste of time. "Not a real job," he always said. He refused to let me go to the Art Academy, and then he forced me to go to work as soon as I left school. I started off working in the hills of Carrara.'

'And now?' Her gaze was intense and his guilt doubled.

'Now I work in an office all day.'

'So, you are from Carrara?'

'I was born in Florence, but I've travelled a bit.' That was true enough. Nic pointed to the fountain in the courtyard beside them. 'I love to paint when I get time but, as you know, it is necessary to work.'

Gia's narrowed eyes—or it could be the fact that she couldn't see him properly—appeared to be assessing him.

'So, what do you paint?'

'Still-life compositions—but in a natural setting. It's not just a hobby— it's my passion, and I do it well enough. My main problem is finding the time.' He turned his hands over and held out his palms. 'I promised my mother before she died that I wouldn't let my art go. So here I am . . . a summer holiday down here with no distractions.'

Gia was staring at him and taking in every word he said. She was certainly a pleasant interruption, and he didn't want her to think otherwise.

Settling back against the stone seat, he took care in choosing the right words. 'You rebel by pretending to be the person your parents want you to be. I accepted what was expected of me, and that makes me admire your passion even more.'

'How did you know what I do?' Gia tipped her head to the side. 'Was it because you saw my landscapes on the wall? I'm surprised Papa told you.'

Nic picked up her hand closest to him and held it up. 'Scarlet fingers? The smell of turpentine?' He grinned at her. 'A dead giveaway. Unless you are a house painter?'

'You *are* astute, aren't you? I paint every day,' she said simply.

'And that's how I've sold out my passion.' Nic's voice turned bitter as memory flooded through him. 'I spend my days working and my art falls away—a little more every year. When my father refused to help me go to the Academy, I rebelled in my own way.'

'How?'

Nic raised his hand and traced the word that was tattooed on his chest behind his shirt.

Coraggio.

Courage. The simple word in a black fancy-flowing script was centred on his chest.

'When my father said I had to . . . work in the quarry I was devastated.' He stared over the low wall in front of them. Lazy spirals of smoke rose in the sky from the small cottages scattered around the valley. 'My mother understood, and she didn't put it down to teenage moodiness. She took my brother and me on a short trip to the countryside to meet a friend. At the time we just put it down to her quirky nature and went along for her. We missed a couple of days of school, so we weren't going to argue.'

She chuckled. 'And?'

Nic grinned at the memory. He could think of his

wonderful mother without the searing grief these days. 'Mamma was into astrology. Her gypsy friend read my palm and made up a chart for me. We ignored her mutterings about moons and planets rising, but when she asked Mamma if she could tattoo my chest I was stoked. Wow, how way cool was that to a sixteen-year-old?'

Nic stared at Gia. He could still remember the coal-black eyes of the gypsy woman burning into his as she'd read his palm, and her mutterings about him finding his destiny in this very countryside. 'So now I am finding the time—and the courage—to follow my dream as best I can. I owe it to my mother's memory.'

'I'm sorry to hear she has gone. But what a wonderful way to remember her.'

He nodded. 'It is. She was a beautiful person, inside and out. I miss her every day.'

And every day when he looked at his tattoo, Nic felt more and more distant from his dream, but he wasn't going to share that. He picked up Gia's hand in his. 'So, if I can help you achieve *your* dream, even in a small way, it would make me happy.'

He looked down in surprise as Gia squeezed his fingers sympathetically. 'We are a fine pair, aren't we?'

'Selfishness my father calls it. Come on, I'll drop you

home.' He stood and pulled her to her feet. 'Otherwise, neither of us is going to get any work done.'

Her hand stayed in his as they walked back across to the car. It felt good.

'Is this your car?' Her voice was curious as they reached the sports car. 'I didn't get a good look at it this afternoon. I was too busy being angry.'

Nic thought quickly. 'No, I rented it for my holiday.'

'It's very nice.' Gia opened the door and slipped into the passenger side. 'You'd better hope it doesn't rain. The summer storms can roll up the valley very quickly.'

'Yeah, that storm this afternoon almost caught me.' Nic had been staring at the blank canvas when the thunder had rolled in, and he'd run down and moved the Morgan into the garage. The rain had only lasted a few minutes.

He started the car but turned to Gia before he pulled out onto the road. 'Thanks for keeping me company tonight. I enjoyed your company.'

'Would you like to come in for a while when we get back to my place?' Gia's words fell over each other as she rushed on. 'Just to maybe . . . just to see some of my . . . work. Most of it is in the cottage. You'll probably be disappointed, and then you can forget about it.'

Chapter Eight

Nic's chest felt as though he'd been hit by an uppercut coming in low from an unseen assailant. He took a deep breath and looked around as awe filled him from head to toe. An unfamiliar feeling consumed him as he looked at Gia's work while she stood quietly beside him in the huge studio at the back of her cottage. Canvas after canvas lined the walls and Nic walked over to the back wall and pulled a large one to the front. It was obscuring at least another dozen paintings. Walking around the room, he was aware of Gia's wide-eyed gaze fixed on him as he looked at each landscape. Bold strokes and intense colour, with fine detail embedded in each piece; she was a brilliant artist. Colourful fields of lavender, scarlet poppies, burgundy geraniums, and a storm landscape that Nic stood in front of for a full five minutes without speaking, absorbing the emotion that hit him square in the chest.

Boiling purple clouds over a field of lavender shaded in a deeper colour; jagged silver streaks of lightning split the sky. In the far distant background, a woman sat on a stone wall, her hair whipped up by the wind. It had a supernatural sense to it and it was breathtaking.

I must have it. What he could do for Gia filled his mind

and he sought the right words.

Nic turned and looked at her, trying to reconcile this quiet, sweet woman with the passionate artist whose emotions filled the canvases. He struggled to find the right words and finally, Gia's soft voice filled the silence.

'You don't like my work?' She turned to the small kitchenette behind the sink where dozens of pots were filled with paintbrushes. The disappointment in her voice jolted Nic back into the present. He hurried across the studio and gently turned her around as she reached for the coffeepot. Her muscles were rigid, and he realised how nervous she was. *How could she not see the brilliance of what she had created?*

'Please pardon my language, but Gia, but your work is *fottutamente fantastico*.' He lifted her from her feet and hugged her. 'You inspire me. Your work speaks to me just like it did in the restaurant. It moves on the canvas. I can see the flowers swaying in the breeze and I can smell them. I heard the thunder in that big one—' Nic shook his head. Words failed him. 'All I can say is that you have the most perfect technique of any artist I have ever seen. Your work touches me here.' He put her down gently and took her hand in his and placed it on his chest. 'You have a rare and amazing talent.' Nic caught his breath as he looked down at Gia. Her eyes were awash with tears and he reached his thumb up gently and wiped them away. 'Are the tears because you're upset? Were you so nervous about what I would think of your work?'

His words broke through the emotion that was hanging between them and Gia stepped back, brushing the back of her hand across her eyes.

'Give me a minute and I'll go and put my glasses back on so I can see if you really mean what you say.' Her voice shook and she crossed back to the small kitchen and leaned over the countertop with her back to him. Nic watched Gia as she tipped her head back, removed the sole lens and then reached down for her spectacles. Her skirt hit mid-thigh and he let his eyes wander down her legs to her shapely calves. He hadn't noticed how long her legs were.

'I really mean it,' he said as Gia crossed the room and stood beside him. Her cheeks were flushed and her eyes were alive. Her lips parted softly as she stared at him and Nic resisted the urge to lower his head and capture them with his. He was teetering on a thin edge here and he didn't want to scare her. 'Are you telling me that no one else has ever seen these?'

Her head shook slowly from side to side as she held his gaze.

'No one? Ever?' Nic ran his hand through his hair as he searched for the right words.

Gia bit her lip and shook her head again.

'Would you be willing to have an exhibition?' Nic couldn't believe that this magnificent talent was hidden away on an old farm in the countryside. No wonder she wanted to move to Florence.

'Of course. That's my dream but I can't afford it. And I also don't think my work is good enough. There are so many artists who paint the Tuscan countryside. Just go down to the village and look at the shops in the *Via della Volte.* Prints, calendars, wall plaques. I'm just one of hundreds of artists who paint the same thing every year.'

'That's not true, Gia. Your talent is fresh and different. I know we've just met, but I want you to trust me.' Nic ran his hands slowly up Gia's bare arms until his fingers gripped her shoulders gently. 'I want to help you. You can't hide your talent away.'

Gia shook her head and went to speak but Nic put his finger on her lips.

'*Ssh.* Hear me out. I've been working long enough to get some money behind me'—now that *was* a white lie— 'if you'll let me help you set up your exhibition, I can lend you the money to get it advertised and organised. Then when you sell your paintings, you can pay me back.'

'But where would I hold it?' Gia frowned. 'I can't leave Castellina.'

'What's wrong with right here?' Nick gestured to the studio around them. There were three huge stone walls where canvases could be displayed and the space was huge. He imagined the light in the daytime would be amazing with that south-facing window. 'You've got that beautiful courtyard outside where you could serve refreshments, and I could help you clean up the studio and set up the exhibition.' His business mind kicked in, already he was thinking of the logistics of such an event and how to advertise it in Florence, who to invite. 'Tuscany is the tourist centre of the country. How many Florentines have villas that they use on a weekend? You have a captive market here. A *wealthy* market. All it would take is some advertising, some well-placed invitations and I guarantee you a hugely successful exhibition. A village girl with an amazing talent.' Already he could see the mock-ups of an advertising campaign in his head.

Gia stepped away from him. 'But when? How long are you here on holidays? Would we leave it and organise it for when you come back here next summer . . . that is if you come back next year?' Her brow wrinkled and Nic watched as her finger pushed her spectacles back up when they slid down her nose. He was getting to like that little quirky habit. He was getting to like this quirky woman.

'No. I have some . . . er . . . contacts in Florence. I often spend my weekends there and it's not far to come down here. But I can get it organised for when I am still here.''

'No.' Nick's excitement plummeted as she shook her head with a frown. 'I have always wanted to make my own way. For too long others have been telling me what to do.'

His mind raced. He had to convince her. This was one opportunity that he couldn't afford to let go.

'How can I convince you? How long will it take you working as a waitress to get to Florence? To hire a space for a show?'

'I don't know.' Her voice was a little less determined.

'Look.' He pointed around the room. 'If you just let me help you, you have enough paintings in here to sell to get you straight to Florence, and your days of waitressing will be over. Almost immediately. I can just give you a little startup, and you can pay me back afterwards.'

'I don't know if I'm ready for anyone else to see what I do. Those little landscapes were an experiment. They've been in the restaurant for months and no one has ever wanted to buy them before you. And what if I don't sell any? Then I'll owe you as well as trying to save.' She shook her head with a smile. 'I'll still be waitressing when I am an old woman. And still in Castellina.'

I'm not surprised. Her father hadn't exactly been

forthcoming when he'd enquired about them. But, despite her words, Nic could sense a weakening in her tone.

'How badly do you want to make enough money to move to Florence?' Although he couldn't see how moving to Florence would improve Gia's work. It was perfection just as it was. He was just dangling the carrot to get her to agree to let him help her. He wanted to help her; her work was brilliant and it would be an excuse to spend some more time with this interesting woman.

'Very much.' She lifted her chin.

'Then trust me. I'm willing to help you.' He laughed and lifted her from her feet again. 'Think of me as a sponsor. I was going to say mentor, but I can't possibly say that. Your work is brilliant. You have no need of a mentor.'

'Oh, Nic. Do you really mean it? This is the most exciting thing that's ever happened to me.' Gia's eyes were wide and the frown disappeared as her lips tipped up into a huge smile. 'But you won't be sponsoring me, I'll pay you back whatever you spend.'

Unexpectedly she leaned into him and touched her lips to his in a light kiss. A kiss as light as the brush of a butterfly's wing. The storm that raced through Nic's body was even more unexpected than the kiss. Oh, he'd wanted her from the start; there was no doubt about that. But he'd not expected such an innocent gesture to move him so deeply.

'You are very kind, and I promise I will think about it.' Her breath stirred against his lips as she pulled back and he reluctantly let go of her. His arms had gone around her as she had leaned into him.

Her breath stirred against his lips as she pulled back and he reluctantly set her back on her feet.

'My pleasure.' Since she'd kissed him, Nic's body was trying to kick into an entirely different type of pleasure. The touch of her soft lips on his had been everything he'd expected and more. He had to fight against crushing Gia to him and deepening the kiss. 'It's time I went home.'

She looked up and the expression in her eyes rocked him. His blood pulsed hot and fast through his veins.

'Thank you for sharing your work with me… for trusting me,' he said, freezing as Gia took a step toward him and put one hand onto his cheek. With her other hand, she reached up and he waited for her to push those spectacles up but she slowly pulled them off and threw them onto the sofa beside them. She stretched up to her toes and her lips touched his . . . again, a whisper of a kiss, but when she pressed soft kiss after kiss against his mouth, his control disappeared.

'You have touched me with your kindness.' She stretched up to her toes and her lips touched his . . . again, a whisper of a kiss.

His control slipped and he pulled her close so that her body was pressed hard against his. That damn strawberry fragrance was everywhere. Need reared in him.

He moved his hand to her waist and his thumb brushed the bare inch of skin between her T-shirt and her skirt. Her kiss had been sweet, but he knew there was passion that simmered beneath; the feeling in her paintings was a part of her. Sweet was not the right word for this woman. Running his hand around her waist and up her spine, Nic cupped his fingers around the back of Gia's slender neck, her skin smooth beneath his fingers. He held her head still and captured her lips, and this time there was no sweetness in her response. Her mouth opened beneath his as he increased the pressure and held her close. Her soft breasts were crushed against his chest as she wrapped her hands around his neck. Fire raced along Nic's veins, and he deepened the kiss, meeting her tongue with his. She lifted her foot and wound her leg around his calf as he drank her in. He loved the way she clung to him as though she wanted to touch him with every part of her body. The fire continued lower and reluctantly he pulled back a little. Despite the way she was returning his kiss, Nic didn't want to frighten her. He lifted his head as he stepped back but kept his hands on her smooth skin. Her T-shirt had lifted a little, and his fingers brushed the bare skin at her waist. Smooth and silky. So tempting to ask where the bedroom was and drag her there, but that was not why he was here.

Not yet. That could come later . . . if that was what Gia wanted.

Chapter Nine

Gia woke early the next morning and stretched. Her legs brushed against the smooth cotton sheets and she snuggled into the soft mattress, a smile tilting her lips. When she had brushed that light kiss across Nic's lips, she had no idea of the passion that simmered below his casual exterior. He had kissed her senseless last night. He'd run his lips across her cheeks, down her neck, and touched the sensitive spot he'd discovered behind her ear. They'd both been breathless when he'd pulled back and called a halt before things had got out of hand. Nic had held her gently, winding his fingers tenderly through her hair as they'd both caught their breath. All of Gia's worries had disappeared like the morning mist evaporating in the soft morning sun.

She'd walked him to his car, and another ten minutes had been spent in his arms and Gia had gasped as his fingertips had gently stroked her skin.

'Can I come back tomorrow?' Nic had asked, in his husky, altogether-too-sexy voice. As if she would've said no. She'd nearly said, 'You can stay until tomorrow,' but commonsense had prevailed. She'd only known him for a few hours, and it was way too soon.

When he had driven off down the dark road, she regretted

her decision. Being with him made her feel alive, and it wasn't just that he'd admired her work. It had more to do with the way Nic made her feel, more than the promises he had made about helping her. He had seen the real Gia, and he respected her for the person she *was*.

She had to think about his offer. Was it the solution to her problem? Could she really accept the faith he had in her work?

But a show that he loaned her the money for? Gia frowned; it was too much to organise and she would feel uncomfortable about Nic paying the costs. What if she didn't sell anything? Maybe Papa would lend her the money and Nic could help her organise it. The main problem with Papa refusing to fund her move to Florence was that he didn't want her to leave the village. But maybe if she could convince him that this would set her studio up, here in Castellina, selling her paintings, she might stay . . .

But that isn't what I want

There was no point asking Papa. Gabriel had a good business head on his shoulders. Maybe he would listen to her dilemma and give her some advice.

Gia rolled over in bed and put her hand behind the back of her head, looking at the patterns in the weathered timber that formed the ceiling above her bed.

Her grandparent's bed. The old farmhouse had belonged

to her mother's parents and when she'd insisted on moving out into her own place, it was as far as Papa would let her go; and in an attempt to dissuade her from leaving home, he even charged her rent. But it was a perfect studio for her needs, and Gia had converted the whole back living area into a work area by herself. It was her bolt hole from her noisy, vivacious family and they rarely came here to visit. Apart from the restaurant, Papa insisted that they all meet at the family home in the village for lunch every Saturday; the only time the restaurant was closed.

Gia groaned and covered her face. Damn; she'd forgotten today was Saturday. She was expected for lunch in the village at noon. She hoped Nic would arrive early so she could explain she had to leave.

##

Never one to waste time—or an emotion that was bubbling inside of her—Gia was hard at work when the sound of a car pulling up outside came in through the open window. It was a warm summer morning and she'd flung open all of the windows to let the fragrance of the flowers drift through her workspace. The large lavender bush beneath the window filled the room with a heavenly scent, and the farmer next door was cutting hay; the sweet smell of freshly cut hay mingled with the lavender. She put her brush down and pushed her spectacles up on her nose— she still hadn't found her other contact lens. Gia frowned;

knowing the mess her studio was usually in, she'd probably washed it down the sink when she'd rinsed her brushes in her hurry to get to work last night. If she didn't find it, she'd have to take a trip to Siena to get another set. As footsteps crunched on the stones of the narrow path outside her studio, shyness gripped hold of Gia, settling in her stomach like a little clutch of butterflies. Heat ran into her face and she picked up a piece of cardboard lying on her workbench and fanned herself just as there was a tap at the door.

Last night had been exciting; so out of character for her—she was usually reserved in dealing with new acquaintances. Feeling so comfortable with Nic last night had been new for her. But now in the light of day, nerves racked her and the usual uncertainty that plagued her returned tenfold. Walking slowly across to the door, she wiped her hands on her T-shirt and ran her hands through her wild curls, before pulling the door open.

Nic stood there, his expression serious, and Gia's stomach sank. She'd been right to feel uncertain. *Second thoughts in the cold light of day*. Why would anyone want to waste their vacation helping out a stranger? He'd changed his mind. At least she hadn't jumped at his offer to bankroll a show. She would have felt even more embarrassed if she had.

Gia lifted a hand to her face as her skin burned. They stared at each other until a smile spread across his face and his dark eyes crinkled at the corners. His hand appeared from behind his back holding a bunch of yellow roses.

'I saw these in the garden at the villa and I couldn't resist the colour.' He held the flowers out to Gia and she buried her face into the soft, sweet-smelling petals. When she lifted her head, he leaned over and slid his lips slowly across her cheek and Gia's certainty came flying back.

Yes, oh, yes.

'Come in, come in.' She stepped back to let him through the door, and as she pulled it shut, he wandered over to her easel.

'You've started work already?' His smile was sending those butterflies into a frenzy.

'Yes, I have to go out later and I wanted to catch the light.' She wandered over to stand beside him and Nic lifted his arm and draped it loosely around her shoulders as he stared at her painting. A feeling of contentment settled in Gia's bones.

'A new one?'

She nodded.

'It looks happy. I love the way you use that scarlet shade almost as your signature colour.' Nic dropped his arm, and Gia left him looking at the canvas to walk across to the sink. She found an empty jar for the roses.

'You have to go out? I was hoping I could take you out for a picnic lunch and we could talk about your show.' Nic leaned back on the workbench and watched as she arranged the flowers.

Disappointment flooded through her and she grimaced. 'I have to go to my parents' place in the village for our weekly lunch.' The disappointment evaporated as Nic held her gaze, and Gia grinned back at him. Her self-assurance took a huge upswing as he smiled. 'But you know what? I think a business meeting to discuss my show should be a priority today.'

'Are you sure?'

Gia nodded. 'I'll call them in a while and tell them I can't make it today.' She kept her voice positive; this would be the first time that she'd ever missed a family lunch. The only excuse that Papa would take was being too ill to get out of bed. But damn it all, she was a grown woman with her own life to explore . . . and live. She was not going to spend the rest of her life wasting away in this village to be the person Papa wanted her to be. Nic was only here for a short time, and now that she'd gotten to know him a little—if that explosive kiss could be called getting to know him—she was determined to enjoy his company whenever she had the opportunity.

'Last year I went down to Siena and discovered this medieval orchard where they do a great lunch outdoors. Do you know it?' Nic was wandering around the room, looking at her paintings again, one by one and Gia could almost hear the "yes" or "no" as he flicked through the canvases.

'No, I don't.'

'It will be a business lunch. We'll have a formal meeting to discuss my suggestion.' He flicked over another canvas and looked at her quizzically. 'I hope you don't mind me looking at them again?'

'No, no. Look your fill. My sponsor'— she grinned at him— 'can look as much as he likes. He has the final say in my show, you know.'

Nic walked back over to her and slipped his arms around her waist and Gia tipped her head back to look at him. His blue eyes were full of light, and heat pooled in her belly.

'You know, I swore this morning, I'd keep my hands off you, but I didn't last very long, did I? Am I going too fast for you?' he asked softly.

Gia stood on her toes and brushed a kiss across his lips. 'You and I obviously have something going here. You're only here for a few days, so what's the point in going too slow and wasting time?' Gia couldn't believe the words that came out of her mouth.

Nic's arms tightened around her and she stared back at him.

'What about your own painting? You're here early. Have you done any work yet?' she asked.

Nick grinned at her. 'No, there's been this distraction I discovered when I went for dinner last night.'

'Well, Nic . . .' Gia stepped back and put on a mock stern face. 'That's not why you are in Tuscany.'

'But it's a good reason to take the day off. Are you working at the restaurant tonight?' He tipped his head to the side and looked innocent.

'Yes, I am.'

'Then I'll paint tonight. And then I'll come and see you after you get home and tell you what I did.'

Oh, God. Just the playful look on his face was sending little trembles from her lower belly down to her thighs . . . and places in between. She was in trouble here; those butterflies weren't going anywhere.

'Can I ask you a favour?' Gia laid her hands flat on Nic's T-shirt-covered chest. 'If we are going to Siena for lunch, would you mind if we left a little bit earlier? I've got a spare pair of contacts and a new pair of glasses waiting for me there. I can collect them.'

'Sure, not a problem. Do you want to do some more work before we leave?'

Gia left his arms and picked up her phone from the table. 'Let's go now. I'll just call my parents and then I'll get changed.'

'I'll go and check out the garden.' Nic shot her a smile

and wandered outside closing the door behind him. She smiled; it was thoughtful of him to think of her privacy.

Gia dialled the restaurant because she knew her parents would be there, already prepping for the dinner trade tonight before they went home to prepare the usual huge lunch for the family. Gabriel would be there with his latest girlfriend—and his snide comments. Louisa would run in during the break when she closed her leather shop for two hours. It was time their parents realised they all had their own lives. *Ha—as if little meek me would be the one to tell them that.*

The little fragile flower, for goodness' sake. Thinking of what she had overheard her father call her last night reaffirmed her determination to get her message through to him now. This wasn't going to be easy, but she was a grown woman who wanted to go—no, scrub that—who *was* going to Siena for the day—with a man who saw her for who she really was, but she wasn't mentioning *that* to her father.

The phone rang for a long time but Gia looked through the window as she waited for Papa to pick up. Nic leaned on the back wall watching the hay being cut and rolled on the farm beside her land. His long legs were stretched out in front of him and the sunlight gave a bluish glint to his black hair. Gia let the scene imprint on her photographic memory and filed it away for a future landscape. When Nic left she would paint him and have something to look at, even though the thought of him not being around left a hollow ache in her chest.

Already.

The phone kept ringing as she stared at Nic, drinking in her fill. Her father would be waiting for someone else to pick up and then he would remember there was no one else there with him besides Mamma. Papa had his quirks and she loved him dearly, but it was time to stand up for herself.

Way past time.

Finally, his deep booming voice came over the phone. '*Giannino's*.'

'Papa. It's Gia.'

'Hello, *bella figlia*. Are you better? I have been so worried about you.'

'Yes, thank you, I'm fine. I'm ringing to tell you I won't be there for lunch today.'

Silence. *The calm before the storm.*

'You are still sick. I am on my way.'

Gia rushed on before he could disconnect. 'No, no, I am fine, but I must go to Siena. I have to pick up new contact lenses. I have lost one and my spectacles need replacing.' A great explanation came to her. 'I am sure that is why I had a headache last night.' Fingers crossed behind her back for the little white lie that sprang to her lips.

'How are you getting there?'

Irritation burned in Gia's throat. She was twenty-three years old, for goodness' sake. 'With a friend.'

'A friend?'

Her courage ran out and she rushed on. 'Must go, car's outside. Love you, Papa. I'll see you tonight.'

She hit disconnect before he could argue.

***

Ten minutes later they were in Nic's Roadster and heading for Siena. He'd rolled the top of the car down and Gia had tied a scarf that matched her sundress over her loose curls to hold them back.

'Your parents were okay with you cancelling?'

Gia smiled across at him and Nic's heart did a slow heavy flip in his chest. She'd replaced those ugly black spectacles with sunglasses. She looked like a movie star.

Very Audrey Hepburn.

Fresh and young and innocent. He swallowed as he waited for her answer. Last night had rocked him. It had been so hard to leave her, and he'd had to pull back or they would have ended up in her bed. She was a country girl and shy, but her response to his kiss had sent the blood spinning through his body. When he woke up this morning, Gia's beautiful face was the first thing to come into his thoughts. Was he doing the right thing by offering to help her out, or should he just bury himself in his villa, focus on his own painting, and mind his own business? No, it was too good an opportunity to pass up. She had fallen into his lap for a reason. Or almost beneath his car.

Thanks, Mamma.

'Yes, once I explained I wouldn't be able to work tonight unless I went to Siena and went to the optometrist, they were most understanding.' Her smile turned into a cheeky grin.

Nic turned his attention back to the road. The last thing he'd expected when he'd headed for Tuscany was to meet someone like Gia.

As her mentor—or sponsor—he would keep his distance and keep the relationship between them on a purely business level while he organised her exhibition. Because he was sure she would take up his offer. It was an escape plan for her.

Keep control. Sure, he could do that. He'd been doing it all his life.

If Gia knew he was a Baldini from *Casa Marmo*, that he'd lied to her about his identity . . . he didn't know what she'd do.

He regretted not telling her the truth from the start, but—and this was a testament to his own needs—he wanted her to accept his affection and assistance because of his own merits. Not because of the bank accounts behind his name. A talent such as hers could not be hidden away, and he would consolidate his position in the Florentine art world as the mentor who discovered her. The board position would be his for sure.

She fascinated him. She was very different from the women he usually spent time with. For a brief moment, he considered telling her he owned the villa. No, it was better that she didn't know—although at least she'd accept his help more readily because she would know he was wealthy. He shook his head slightly as they approached the *autostrada*. If Gia knew he was a Baldini from *Casa Marmo*, she could end up liking him and wanting him around because of his money. He'd been there before.

He'd forget about that for the day and simply enjoy being in the company of a beautiful, talented . . . and complicated woman.

A woman who attracted him way too much.

Chapter Ten

It was a beautiful clear day in Siena; the sun was warm but not too hot, and the breeze was light. The fragrance of summer blossoms in the air followed Nic and Gia as they walked from the parking lot through the old town to *Piazza del Campo*. Nic had parked the car in the *Fortezza-Stadio* next to the Medicean fortress to avoid a fine in the limited traffic area of the city centre.

Gia stopped into her optometrist; the rooms were conveniently located in an alley behind the *piazza*. She stepped out of the building and looked up and down the narrow, cobbled street for Nic, clutching the bag containing her new contact lens and stylish glasses. The streets were full of tourists dressed in colourful summer clothes and Gia took a deep breath, happiness flooding through her as she enjoyed being a part of this day, away from her usual routine. Nic was nowhere in sight, so she waited outside the building until he appeared.

When he finally came around the corner, his mouth tilted in a wide smile. 'Ready?' He took her arm and led her down an alley, through the edge of the town toward a green area in the middle of the city. 'Come on, lunch is just down here.'

Gia looked ahead of them with interest. Even though they were in the middle of the walled city, a long avenue lined with trees led down the hill to an orchard. Halfway down, the trees gave way to vegetable plots and orange trees. She laughed when a donkey stepped onto the pathway ahead of them and brayed with annoyance as he blocked their way.

'I didn't know this was in the city centre. It's gorgeous.' Gia paused while Nic shooed the donkey on with his free hand. His other hand was low on her back and warm tingles were jolting along her nerve endings every time he increased the pressure of his hand.

'*All'Orto de' Pecci.*' Gia read the sign ahead of them at the entrance to a large garden at the end of the avenue.

'A medieval garden, with great food . . . and wine.' Nic slipped his arm around her waist and they walked over to the outside tables which were covered with a canopy of green leaves.

Gia's smile widened and she leaned into Nic when they reached their table. 'A great place to talk business.'

Life was good.

***

Nic had relaxed by the time they reached the outdoor table that he'd booked while Gia had been collecting her spectacles. Her comment about talking business had sent a shaft of confidence shooting through him. A contented smile parted her lips softly as she looked up at the grape leaves lining the frame that supported the vine. He slid his hand over hers as they sat at the table and focused on her mouth as the tip of her tongue wet her lips.

'I hope it's okay with you. I ordered the lunch buffet that they serve to the table. I know you have to be back in time to work at the restaurant tonight and we need to make some plans. That is if you've decided to take me up on my offer. And if you accept, we have to make some plans.'

For the first time in his life, Nic had met a woman who fascinated him on more than a physical level. If he was looking for a partner, Gia would be the sort of woman he would spend time with, but he would never go down that path. Not after the train wreck his father's life had become after he'd lost Mamma. No social life. No time for his sons. It was as though his life force had died with her.

'That's fine with me. It will be wonderful to be waited on.' Gia's voice was soft and Nic smoothed his thumb over the back of her hand. It was an unfamiliar feeling for him; this need to touch her skin, to feel her warmth, to smell the strawberry fragrance he now realised came from her hair. She'd pulled the colourful scarf from her hair and put it into her bag. Her hair was a mass of wild black curls around her face and Nic's fingers tingled with the need to run his hands through the tangle. He closed his eyes, imagining her hair spread out on a snowy white pillow.

He squirmed in his chair as his jeans suddenly became

tighter around his groin. He hadn't felt a need as urgent as this for a long time and he dropped the linen napkin onto his lap. Gia stared at him, and he cleared his throat, trying to make his voice businesslike.

'Okay, so what have you decided?' Nic cursed himself. He'd meant to ease into the discussion, be gently persuasive and let her come to a positive decision with his subtle encouragement. The way he always did business. The way he'd brought so many export contracts to Baldini Enterprises. But the ache between his legs had caused a short circuit in communication between his brain and his mouth.

'Yes.' Her voice was soft.

'Yes?' Nic couldn't believe what he was hearing. 'Yes, to "let's put on an exhibition of your work"'?'

'Are you really sure you want to help me with this?' Gia's eyes were huge. She'd flipped the sunglasses back to hold her hair from her face.

'Do you think you could find thirty canvases that you would be happy to show? We need your first show to be representative, with enough of a range to get the buyers interested.'

'My first show?' The expression on her face was one of shock, and a surge of guilt ran through him. It was so hard to reconcile the unassuming woman in front of him with the artist who painted with such emotion.

Before he could answer, she rushed on and her words ran together. 'Nic, I want you to know something before we say any more. Okay?'

'Okay.' He nodded and waited, wondering what she was thinking.

'My feelings for you have nothing to do with my art. It is a lovely, shall we say, a bonus. But if you were to decide not to help me, I'd still like you. Still be attracted to you. I need you to know that.'

Gia *was* honest, without artifice, and that fired Nic's interest in her even more. Knowing she liked him, the real Nic, for what he was, without knowing anything about his wealth or his power, or what he could do for *her,* made his chest swell with a warmth that he was not used to. He didn't want to disillusion her with his identity. Things were fun between them as they were.

Had it only been yesterday that he'd met her? It seemed as though he'd known her for months. Surely, one didn't come to know a person in scant hours. Yet, he could anticipate her every quirk: the way she pushed her spectacles up, the way she wet her lips when she was unsure, and the wicked sense of humour that appeared in funny little comments when he was least expecting them.

She had him enthralled. This seemingly shy woman whose art showed a passion at odds with the way she presented herself to the world. 'Thank you, and yes, the first of many.' He squeezed her hand. 'I'll help you get ready.'

'Oh, I'm ready.' That damned tongue made an appearance again, and Nic looked away, relieved to see the waiter approaching with a bottle of water.

'So, how long will it take us to clear up your studio?'

'Not long. There's another building close by. I can get Gabriel to help.' Gia stopped and rolled her eyes. 'You know my family is going to think this is the most stupid thing ever.'

'And that bothers you?' As Nic watched Gia straightened in her chair and her face lost its softness.

She straightened—another quirk, this one when she felt threatened—and her face lost its softness. He reached for her hand and brushed his thumb over the soft skin on the inside of her wrist.

'Talk to me,' he said. The thought of anyone putting down this woman . . . it enraged him.

'No,' she said softly. 'It would have once, but I'm ready to move on. And if this all works out, as soon as I pay you back and I have enough money left, I'll move to Florence. But there's one thing I insist on.'

'What's that?'

'A written agreement. Because I will pay you back every cent.'

The last thing he wanted was for her to see his last name on a document. He'd gone to great lengths to book the table in another name, and he'd paid for the buffet when she was getting her glasses, so she wouldn't see Baldini on his card. He'd sort something out, but for now, he'd agree.

'Okay. I'll get that sorted. Now let's settle on a date.'

He outlined what they needed to do as their lunch was served.

'You are so organised. And you know so much.' Gia's laugh warmed him and her enthusiasm was infectious. She shook her head as he rattled off priorities and the order in which they needed to do them, and he laughed back with her.

'The only thing you have to worry about is your paintings. Leave the rest to me. Okay?'

She nodded. 'That's the easy part.'

And it is to her. That came as naturally to her as the planning and organisational skills came to him, although he listened, surprised as she recited the thirty canvases she was going to show without hesitation.

Nic suggested a starting price, and her mouth dropped open.

'No way.'

He shook his head slowly. 'You are such a babe in the woods, Gia. Of course, your work is worth that—probably more. We'll bring in a professional appraiser.'

Now it was Gia's turn to shake her head. 'No, I can't afford that.'

Frustration bit at Nic, frustration he couldn't just say that this is the way we'll do it. And that he would pay for everything. She would owe him nothing, but he couldn't afford to scare her off. He still couldn't believe his luck in finding her. Mamma was up there looking out for him; if it hadn't been for the promise to her, he'd still be sitting in his office in Carrara.

'I don't want this to get out of hand. Just a few of my canvases on display, invite a few people and we'll see what happens…and then take it from there.'

Nic smothered a grin. He'd already thought of the people he would invite. She was in for a big surprise. And so were they.

She pushed her plate away. 'Let's make this day perfect.'

'Here?' The words were out of his mouth before he could think, and Gia's laugh tinkled softly around him.

'So, what would make it perfect for you, Nic?' The wide eyes staring at him did not belong to the meek waitress he'd rescued from the road. Nic's mouth dried as the sultry temptress sitting opposite him waited for him to answer.

'No. You go first.' Nic waited as her lips tipped into a

smile. Her gaze ran over his body, and he could swear it was like her warm fingers touching him.

'Ice-cream.' She burst out laughing at the look on his face. 'We'll seal the deal with ice-cream.'

'Not quite the dessert I had it mind, but I can live with ice-cream if it makes your day perfect.'

He summoned the waiter and when they ordered, Nic avoided the strawberry. He had to get himself back in control. He let Gia order and as they shared a bowl of different flavours of *gelato,* he sensed a shift in her. A quiet determination that hadn't been there before, and he wondered if it was the thought of the exhibition, or whether her thoughts were following the same path as his. *All the way to her bedroom.* Or even better— one day—his bedroom at *Casa Marmo.* For a moment, he imagined her hair spread on the decadent bed against the scarlet of the covers. The mirrors reflected every nuance of her face, every curve of her body.

'What are you thinking about?' Her voice was soft, and Nic brought himself back to the present.

'Food.' He swallowed. 'I have some connections in restaurants in Florence.' It wasn't the time to tell her that he actually owned three small restaurants around the *Piazza della Signoria* near the Uffizi Gallery.

She wrinkled her nose. 'Papa will be upset if I hire

someone else for the food.'

'We'll keep it simple,' he said. 'A couple of waiters mixing discreetly with trays of champagne and some canapés. That's all you need. I'll go and see your father and suggest the idea.'

Gia's face lit up and her eyes were full of amusement. 'I know. I'll get Gabriel to serve the champagne. He'll *love* that.'

Chapter Eleven

Gia sighed as Nic parked the car at her gate. A pleasant sleepiness had been helped along by the warmth of the mid-afternoon sun and the smooth purr of the sports car. It had been the most wonderful day and the last thing she wanted to do was work at the restaurant. She was not looking forward to slipping back into the old Gia mindset and putting her head down and quietly going about her work. The excellent meal was way more than she ever ate for lunch. In fact, most days she didn't eat if she was painting. A wide yawn escaped her.

Nic glanced across at her as she stayed sitting in the car. 'Tired?'

They'd shared a bottle of wine with lunch and Gia had had more than her share because Nic was driving. A pleasant buzz accompanied the warmth from the mid-afternoon sun.

'A little. I might have to have a rest before I go to the restaurant. I can't have the wobbles when I'm serving.' She looked at him from beneath her lashes. 'Would you like to come inside for a while?'

Something unspoken passed between them as their eyes met and held. Gia shivered and the delicious tremor that ran through her as Nic's steady gaze pinned her turned into a physical need. He held his hand out, and she felt like a princess as she reached up and he helped her out of the car. Keeping her hand in his, she led him across the lawn and pushed open the door of the cottage.

'Not locked?' Nic's breath was warm against her neck and she shivered.

Gia lowered her voice as she shook her head. 'No need, it's safe here. Nobody ever comes this way.'

Nic followed her inside and she stood by the door for a moment, uncertain if he understood what she was offering. She dropped his hand and clenched her fingers as she closed the door behind them, trying to stay calm. Her knees loosened and a tremble ran down her legs when he stepped closer to her. Gia tipped her head back and sighed as Nic leaned over and held her, his hands gentle on her bare arms. He lowered his head and pressed a kiss to her neck, moving his lips slowly up and onto her cheek. His lips left a trail of fire on her skin as her blood beat slow and heavy through her body. Gia unclenched her fingers and turned slowly to face him. His eyes held hers and her breath hitched at the desire she saw in his expression. Warmth pulsed through her. Her body seemed to have a mind of its own, never before had she responded so powerfully to a man. Her fingers ached with the need to touch him, to feel the muscles outlined by his T-shirt, to run her hands down his back and linger on his bare skin.

The butterflies began to flutter in Gia's stomach as they stood and looked at each other. With a deep groan, he reached for her, threading his fingers through her hair and pulling her close. His mouth closed on hers, hot and hard. An unfamiliar feeling tingled between her thighs and her nipples hardened against the soft cotton of his T-shirt as she opened her lips.

God, she wanted him so much. Reaching around to the back of his neck, Gia held Nic close and pressed her body against his so he was in no doubt as to what she wanted. She lowered her hands and ran her fingers over his hard chest, exploring the ridged muscles and his hard abs, and she closed her eyes when he groaned again. He lifted his mouth from hers and her breath came in soft pants as Nic ran one hand slowly up the inside of her thigh beneath her dress. His fingers were warm and teasing on her bare skin.

Gia held her breath as his hand reached the top of her leg and paused. His eyes held hers and she nodded.

***

The groan that came from Gia when he touched her almost brought Nic undone on the spot. Her body leaned into his; the only sound in the studio was their breathing, hot and heavy. Gia's hand left his chest and played with the button at the top of his jeans.

She pulled her head back and stared at him. 'Have you got a—?'

'In my wallet. In the back pocket of my jeans.' He knew his voice was ragged but for the life of him, he couldn't move. He couldn't think; he was out of control and he didn't care. Nic closed his eyes as he heard his wallet hit the wooden floor an instant before the rip of the foil packet.

His lips nuzzled Gia's neck as her hand went to the waistband of his jeans and her fingers worked their magic. He pulled back and stared at her, her lack of inhibition firing hot desire in him, more powerful than he'd ever experienced before. Her scent surrounded him, the strawberry shampoo mingling with the smell of her intimate fragrance.

Sanity came slowly back to Nic as he caught his breath. Five minutes ago, he'd had every intention of dropping her off and going back to the villa.

They were standing just inside her entry door. But it was too late. The need for completion overcame his doubts when Gia opened her eyes and smiled at him.

He lifted his mouth away from hers and looked deep into her eyes. Her dark brown gaze held his; she was so beautiful, so full of life, so vivacious.

'Are you sure?' Nic closed his eyes, lost in the sensation of the emotion filling his chest.

'I'm sure,' she whispered.

Afterwards, they stood together for several minutes as they each regained their breath, lost in their own thoughts.

Nic was awash with guilt. Even though it had been inevitable from the moment he'd kissed her—and mind-blowing—he still felt as though he'd done the wrong thing, and taken advantage of Gia. Never before had he lost control like that with any woman.

'Are you okay?' He took a jagged breath and rested his forehead against hers.

'*Mmm.*' Gia's lifted her mouth and her lips were soft against his. 'Never better.' She pulled her head back and stared at him. 'I mean it. I have never felt so alive.'

Five minutes later, after Gia had pointed out the bathroom to him, Nic leaned on the basin and stared at himself in the mirror. *What the hell had just happened out there?* Resting his hands on the basin, he stared in the mirror. He had spent the last five years protecting himself from getting close to any woman.

Sure, sex was as necessary to him as food. There had always been a woman he could call on, warm and willing, to take him to her bed. But never before had he felt such a deep desire to claim a woman as his own.

Up until tonight, he'd always been able to indulge, enjoy

and share, and keep his emotions safe, clear, and uninvolved.

No way he was ever going to put himself at the risk of what his father had suffered. Whenever he had sensed he was getting too close to a woman, he had always pulled back.

Hell, he'd lost himself back there, and it scared him to death.

In less than two days, Gia had breached his defences, and she hadn't even tried to. She seemed to want nothing from him, but the power that she could have over him if he let her frightened the hell out of him.

I have control, and that isn't going to change.

***

Gia rearranged her dress, pulled her hair back and secured it with a clip. Her cheeks were still hot and her lips were tender, but she couldn't help the smile that tugged at them. She looked up as Nic came out of her bathroom and her smile grew wider as she let her eyes wander over his tousled hair, his broad shoulders and his muscular chest. But when he looked back at her, a tremor of uncertainty ran through Gia. His eyes were hooded and his mouth was set in a straight line. She turned away before he could see the doubt on her face. Nic followed her and Gia tensed as his hand touched her shoulder and he spun her around gently.

'I think maybe I should apologise to you this time.' Nic's voice was soft and Gia looked back at him, not knowing what she had done wrong. Maybe it hadn't been good for him? She was inexperienced—teenage groping with Stefano, and a couple of unsatisfactory dates in the last couple of years—had not exactly given her a lot of practice in knowing what a man wanted. Embarrassment poured through Gia; she'd practically thrown herself at Nic because a good-looking man had paid some attention to her.

Ha . . . and praised her work. What a huge mistake she'd made. She felt like crawling back into her shell.

What was I thinking?

But trying for nonchalance, she raised her eyebrows as he stared down at her, determined not to let him see her uncertainty. 'Oh?'

'I was like a teenage boy.' He ran his hair through his hair. '*Madre Dio*, we didn't even make it to a horizontal surface. Not very thoughtful of me.'

Relief flooded through Gia. It had nothing to do with her inexperience. She looped her arms around his waist, and Nic lowered his head so that his forehead rested on hers. His breath was warm on her face. She would not let her newfound poise disappear. A confident little chuckle escaped her lips. 'And you think I cared? Who pulled your wallet from your pocket? The tooth fairy? And who—'

'Okay . . . okay . . . yes, you are certainly full of surprises.'

Nic lightly captured her lips with his before deepening the kiss. 'And I like each one of them.' They fit together perfectly, and they explored each other as their need began to build again.

Nic pulled back slowly and shook his head, a strange expression on his face. 'I know you have to go to work soon. Do you want me to drive you to the restaurant? What time do you start?'

Gia turned to look at the clock in the small kitchen and squealed. 'Oh, *Dio*. I can't be late *again*.'

'Get ready and I'll drive you.' Nic grinned as she stepped away. 'We can't have that.'

Chapter Twelve

Nothing could interfere with Gia's good mood. She grabbed Papa's face between her hands after she'd put her bag away and planted a smacking kiss on his cheek. She grinned at the look on his face as his drooping moustache tickled her chin.

'See, Papa? I am well. Very well. You have no need to worry about me.'

'Ah, it is good to see you happy. But are you sure you are well? Your cheeks are still rosy?' Papa frowned at her and Gia grinned back at him.

'Yes, I am well, and I can see properly.' She'd left the ugly black glasses at home and slipped on her new glasses with the square scarlet frames. As well as that, Gia had bought a new black fitted skirt and white shirt in Siena. The look on Gabriel's face, when she'd passed by him in the kitchen, had been worth the money she'd spent.

Gia felt like standing on a table announcing to the restaurant that not only was she having an exhibition but she'd had the best experience of her life that afternoon. She stifled a giggle and Gabriel frowned at her, and she couldn't resist being sassy back to him.

'Oh, sorry Gabe'—she knew he hated the diminutive of

his name— 'I forgot I was supposed to be unhappy.' She dug him in the ribs as she walked past with a tray of cutlery.

The same as when they were children, her big brother had to have the last word. 'You can do outside tonight. That group of authors is out there. And don't be sour, make sure you talk to the customers.'

'Love to.' She sashayed towards the door and she grinned again as his words followed her.

'Make them feel welcome.'

You'd never guess her brother had gone to college to learn how to be a manager.

'Yes, boss.' She laughed as she hurried outside and for a change, the look exchanged between her father and brother did not bother Gia in the slightest.

The restaurant was busy as usual and Gia enjoyed serving the table of women. The enjoyment the authors from the writing retreat took in their meal made the night a pleasure for her. She answered their questions about the local area and intercepted several worried looks between her father and brother as she chatted away with them.

When she was serving the dessert, Gabriel called her over and Gia lowered her eyes to the floor, reverting to her usual demeanour. She'd overdone it tonight: she didn't want Papa delving into the reason for her animated behaviour.

But it was Gabriel who looked at her quizzically. 'Are you all right, Gia?'

She looked up from beneath her lashes with a shy smile and kept her voice soft. 'Yes, why?'

'You are just talking to the customers a lot more.' He waved his hands. 'But I am not angry. That is good. I would like to see more of it.'

Gia nodded and turned away, but Gabriel called her back.

'There is a late customer out on the terrace. Can you take his table, please?'

'Yes, not a problem.' Gia turned away. If talking to the customers made Gabriel more pleasant to her, maybe she should try harder.

As she stepped through the door to the courtyard, she smiled at the women at the writers' table. She paused to speak to them again on her way to the other side of the wide courtyard. They had sampled an unending supply of *Limóncello* and *Vin Santo* with their desserts. Papa had excelled tonight. There were many more desserts than usual, and the women groaned as they stood, but promised to return for another meal as they prepared to trudge back up the hill. 'Bye, Gia. See you tomorrow,' one of the women called out.

Gia waved back and waited for them to cross to the gate in the high rose-covered wall that led to the pathway along the side of the road.

The single table was tucked into a shadowy corner at the back of the courtyard and Gia hurried across with her order pad. The sooner she served this late customer, the sooner she would be out of here tonight and see Nic again. Her heartbeat picked up when she saw the customer sitting at the table Gabriel had directed her to. Nic's slow sexy smile sent a shiver straight to her belly.

'What are you doing here?' She kept her voice low in case Gabriel was hovering nearby.

'I thought I'd come back and ask the lovely waitress who served me last night if she could suggest another special course for me.'

Heat flared into Gia's cheeks as she looked back at him. 'What exactly do you fancy tonight, sir?' She knew her tone was flirtatious and she glanced around at the now empty courtyard. 'I can suggest an excellent dessert after your meal. Maybe I could add chocolate to it?'

She leaned forward and he whispered close to her ear. 'Forget the chocolate, you minx. *You* look beautiful. Good enough to eat.' The hidden meaning in his words sent even more heat spiralling, and she covered her confusion by passing him a menu. She might be feeling a bit more confident but not *that* confident. Maybe she'd taken the wrong meaning of his words.

Her legs trembled as she imagined what Nic hinted.

Papa as usual, despite his size, was as stealthy as *Mou-Mou*, the restaurant cat. Gia didn't hear him coming until his voice boomed beside her. She jumped and dropped her order pad to the cobblestones. She tried to compose herself as she bent to pick it up. *How long had he been there?*

'Gia, you are flushed again. You are not ill?' He turned to Nic. 'Welcome back, sir. It is a pleasure to see you again at our little establishment.' Papa frowned. 'Did you ask Gia about her little drawings? '

Gia rolled her eyes behind her father's back as Nic sat up straight, looking like he'd been caught with his hand in the cookie jar. Papa was overdoing it again.

'No,' Gia said.

'Yes,' Nic said at the same time.

Papa looked from one to the other with a frown and then shook his head. 'Well, Gia when you have taken *Signore* ' he looked at Nic with his eyebrows raised in question.

'Nic. Please call me Nic.'

Her father must be making him feel uncomfortable. God, she stifled a giggle. If only Papa knew. He'd be more than uncomfortable; he'd be run out of the village.

'Nic it is. After you bring Nic's order to the kitchen, I am happy for you to talk to him about your drawings.' Papa leaned across to her and lowered his voice. 'But I think he was just making conversation. Don't you go on talking about your art too much? Don't bore him.'

Gia gritted her teeth when Papa patted her cheek gently, as though she was a small child.

'Okay, *bella*?'

'Yes, Papa.' Her voice was soft.

Obedient as always. One comment and her confidence disappeared in a flash. She slumped her shoulders as her father ambled across to the only other table where guests were still seated, and then jumped as Nic grabbed her hand and held it.

'Get that look off your face.'

'What look?' Temper fired, replacing her disappointment at her father's attitude.

'The look that says your art is worth nothing. Don't let your family dismiss your talent like that.' Nic squeezed her fingers. 'Don't give up so easily.'

Gia stared down at him and shrugged as Nic smiled up at her. Those dark blue eyes sent little jolts along her nerve endings and she pulled her hand away.

'Now go and order me something in the kitchen and come back so we can talk about your paintings—with your father's blessing.'

She held out the menu to him. 'What would you like?'

Nic's steady gaze sent a shiver down her back. His slow, sexy smile was the only answer she got. '*Hmm*. Let me think.'

'Tell me something.' Her pen was poised over the order pad and Gia was surprised to see her hand shaking. 'Please.'

Nic tilted his head to the side. 'Well, seeing as I enjoyed a wonderful meal at lunchtime with a beautiful woman, I'm not really very hungry.'

'Okay, how about a small pizza?' Gia fought the smile that was pulling at her lips.

'Small would be good, and that will save room for the dessert I have in mind later.'

Oh my God. Gia's knees were trembling so much that she barely made it across the courtyard back to the kitchen. She slipped the order up on the board and turned to go back outside but Gabriel blocked her way.

'Gia, there's a group upstairs who needs some attention. I'll take over in the courtyard.'

Gia turned to follow her brother's directive as she always did. Took two steps towards the stairs and then stopped.

'No.' She turned back to face her brother. 'Papa asked me to talk to *Signore* Battistoni—the customer from last night. He wants to buy my paintings.'

There! She'd said it and she waited for Gabriel's usual argument but to her surprise, he looked at her intently and then nodded.

'Battistoni?' He looked from her across to Nic and frowned.

'Yes, he was here last night, too, and he likes my paintings.' There was no need to tell him that Nic had seen more than the landscapes on the wall here. What she did away from work was *her* business.

Gabriel paused, his gaze darting between her and Nic. After a few seconds, he nodded. 'Hmm, Battistoni? Very well. I'll handle upstairs.' He kept his gaze on Nic as he crossed to the stairs.

Gia's mouth dropped open as Gabriel bolted up the stairs.

What a day for surprises.

With a smile on her face, and anticipation filling her chest, she walked back out to the courtyard.

***

As Nic expected, Gia argued about the amount he said the four small landscapes on the wall in the restaurant were worth. In the end, she sat at the table with him, and they negotiated a figure agreeable to both of them. He grinned. She didn't have a chance. Her paintings were outstanding, and he wouldn't let her dismiss them for less than the value they deserved.

'So, we're agreed?' He held out his hand across the table. She reached across, took his hand, and he shook it in a businesslike handshake. She removed her hand and pushed her chair back. He reached for his wallet and she shook her head. 'Give it to Papa when you pay the bill. My bag is in the kitchen, and I still have to clear some tables. It's been a pleasure doing business with you.' Gia removed her hand from his and pushed her chair back. 'Now I must go and help finish up in the kitchen.'

'Can I wait for you and drive you home?' He knew he should go back to his villa, but the thought of spending more time with Gia appealed more than the blank canvas. Just spend time with her, maybe watch her paint. Nothing more, no matter how much he had teased her about dessert. It was all business between them from now on. They had done the first deal.

'That would be nice.' A lock of her curls fell and brushed against his face as she leaned down to whisper to him. 'Wait up around the corner at the top of the hill. I'll walk up there. But I'll be an hour or more.' The smell of strawberry shampoo swamped him as Gia frowned. 'If you want to go back to the villa, you don't have to wait around.'

'I'll be there.'

***

Mauro took the four landscapes down from the wall while Nic waited. He paid his bill in cash for the second night running, and he'd made sure he had enough cash in his wallet to pay for the paintings. There was no sign of Gia as her father placed the cash in an envelope for her, before slipping it into the pocket at the front of his apron.

'I'll collect them tomorrow when I am going straight home.' There was no sign of Gia, and he didn't want to look as though he was waiting for her.

'You're going out for the evening? There won't be much open in the village now.' Mauro frowned as he walked to the door with Nic.

He covered up his discomfort with a cough. He knew Gia didn't want her family to know her business. 'Er . . . just for a drive. It's such a nice evening.'

'Thank you very much for your purchase.' Mauro folded his arms across his ample stomach. 'But I do think you have been way too generous for Gia's little hobby.'

'Mauro, surely I'm not the first person to offer to buy Gia's landscapes?'

The older man shrugged. 'No.'

So why had he been willing to discuss her art now, why with him?

Mauro gave another shrug. A cryptic pursing of his lips. '*Buona sera*.'

Nic looked at him curiously. He would do his best to convince Gia of her talent over the next few days; and when he launched her into the art fraternity in Florence, her doubts would disappear.

Especially when she was mentored by the newest member of the Board of Trustees of the Uffizi Gallery.

A young artist beneath my wing. And perhaps in my bed. He couldn't understand his attraction to Gia. He could still feel her slim body pressed up against his. He was used to having beautiful women on his arm—confident women who knew their place in the world. She intrigued him. He understood her passion for her art, and he appreciated her amazing talent. What she put onto the canvas made him realise that his commitment to his art was nowhere near as strong as it could be. Nic loved to paint, and he loved to see the final products, but for him, his creations were structured like his business plans. He was never totally lost in it. His self-control was legendary, even while painting. He was always thinking and planning as he worked on his canvases.

What he craved was to see Gia in action. He wanted to watch as she got those intense emotions onto the canvas.

What did being taken over by the creative muse look like for her? Nic frowned. Maybe he could learn something from her. How ironic would that be? All Gia wanted was to go to Florence to learn, and Nic was pretty sure he could learn more from her in a week at her studio than he would ever have learned at the Academy.

How she worked. The intensity of her expression while

she worked. And that made him think of this afternoon and the expression on her face as they'd made love. Just thinking about being with her, in the entryway of her old cottage, was causing another physical reaction. Fortunately, the courtyard was softly lit. Never before had a woman filled his thoughts and his senses like this. The new studio and his paintbrushes waiting for him back at the villa were far from his mind.

Nic strolled out to the car and looked up into the night sky. It was clear, and the brilliance of the myriad of stars lightened the velvet darkness of the deep blue. The colours of the night touched him and to his deep relief, he now knew what he would paint on those waiting canvases.

Later.

Chapter Thirteen

Nic didn't have to wait long before Gia ran up the hill and stood beside the Roadster. Her hair was in disarray and there was a smudge of something on her chin. Nic stood beside her, reached up and tucked her hair behind her ear and when she turned her lips into his palm, it sent an electric jolt up his arm. She was full of surprises.

'What would you like to do now?' He pulled her closer. 'Ice-cream? Or go straight home?'

'Home, please.' Gia leaned into him and Nic rested his chin on the top of her head. 'I need to paint.' She pulled back and looked at him, her eyes dark and wide. 'Did you notice the stars? I have this idea—'

'Yes, I did . . . and so do I.' Nic smiled. They were on the same wavelength. 'And I was thinking. I would like to watch you work. Would you mind? I understand if you prefer to be alone.'

Gia's laugh rang out in the still night air. 'I would be happy to have the company. It gets very lonely at times.'

'Come on, then. I'll take you home.'

'Sometimes I paint all night, so you don't have to stay if you would prefer to go back to your villa.' Suddenly her shyness touched Nic deep inside.

'I want to stay. Even if it means all night.' In fact, he couldn't think of anywhere he'd rather be.

***

Nic smiled when they walked into Gia's cottage. She strode ahead of him, straight past the wall where they had spent a very enjoyable half an hour earlier. She pointed to the table in the small kitchenette.

'Make yourself at home. I'll just get changed.' Before she walked into the bedroom, she pulled an envelope from her pocket and held it up. 'Thank you very much.' Her voice was shy. 'Papa gave it to me. You do know you are my first customer ever, don't you?'

'I'll be the first of many, you wait and see.'

Gia grinned and disappeared into the other room. Nic walked around the room slowly, looking at the canvases. He would never get tired of looking at her work. The colours she used were incredible.

'Would you like a coffee or a drink?'

Nic turned as she came out of the bedroom. She'd changed quickly into a cropped T-shirt and a pair of loose cotton pants that sat low on her hips. She moved quickly around the room picking up brushes and filling jars with water. Nic sensed her eagerness to begin and knew that she would be the same whether he was here or not. He was used to women fawning over him and knowing that she accepted but pushed aside his presence was a new feeling.

'No, I'm fine. You just do whatever you'd normally do and I'll watch you work.'

'Nic?' Gia tipped her head to the side and Nic watched as the tip of her tongue touched her top lip.

'Have you had a chance to do any painting yet? You seem to have been looking after me ever since I stepped in front of your car.'

He shook his head.

'If you'd like to . . . if you wouldn't mind—' Her voice trailed off and he stared at her. Maybe she was going to send him home after all, but she rushed on as she leaned her elbows on the long bench between them. 'I know you're not in your place, but if you'd like to use one of my canvases and my paint, you're more than welcome.'

Nic looked over at the easel which held her half-completed painting. There were two other easels in different parts of the room. Each was situated beneath a large window. The tingling that had buzzed though his fingertips when he'd been waiting for Gia at the top of the hill returned and he nodded slowly. 'That's very generous of you. I might just take you up on that—after I watch you work for a while.'

He pulled up a chair and sat away from Gia as she stood

and looked at the painting she'd begun that afternoon. She chatted away to him as she mixed colours on the old wooden board on the bench.

'Why do we paint, Nic?'

'What do you mean?'

Gia brushed her hair back with the back of her hand and the first smudge of paint stained her cheek. Nic smiled as she looked down at him. He was leaning back with his legs sprawled out in front of him. It was the most relaxed he'd been for many months. No business pressure, no one calling him wanting decisions made, and best of all, spending time with this fascinating woman.

'This is why I want to go and learn. I know what I feel and I know I must paint, but why do we express ourselves with images rather than words? You know, like that group of women in the restaurant tonight.' She turned and stared through the window. 'They were laughing and having fun, but the intensity of their conversation, when they were talking about their books, reminded me of how I feel when I think about my work.'

Her forehead wrinkled into a frown as she stared at him. 'And then I think of Papa's—and my family's—attitude and think, am I kidding myself to even think of it as work?'

She turned to the canvas and stroked a bold slash of scarlet in the centre. Her voice dropped lower. 'That's why I want to go to the Academy. To understand *why*.'

Nic leaned forward. 'I don't know if I can really call myself an artist, but for me, when I look at a piece of art, it speaks to me.'

Gia nodded as he stared at the canvas. 'That good old— what is the English word? — I have it! That good old chestnut— a picture paints a thousand words.'

'I guess it is the way we express our true selves. Are you familiar with Picasso's words?' Nic asked.

Gia took her attention from the canvas and turned to him. 'Words or works?'

'Words. He once said, "I experience a period of frightening clarity in those moments when nature is so beautiful."' Nic pushed himself to his feet and picked up a brush and looked around for the other palette he had noticed earlier. 'That's what it's like for me. Art lets me express what I see, in a way that I can't put into words.'

Gia had turned back to the canvas and Nic watched as the brush quickly filled in the few white areas left. 'That's why I want to study. To learn all those sorts of things. To find a reason for what drives me.'

'I don't think you need to go to college to find that out. You have it already, Gia. To paint the way you do is to show a little bit more of your soul in every painting you do.' Nic picked up the palette and moved across to the easel near the highest window. He could see the night sky from there. 'How do you feel when you have finished a painting and you stand back and look at it?'

'Outside of it. In a way, I hate the feeling. It is confusing for me. Everything I've put down on the canvas is there in front of me. It's me but it's not *in* me anymore. It takes a while after I finish before I can look at what I've done and see past what I feel, and actually see the picture I've created.'

Gia stepped back and looked at him as Nic began to mix his colours. 'Thank you. You have no idea how good it is to talk to you like this.'

'My pleasure And I'm looking forward to getting your exhibition together. Tomorrow I'll make some calls and we'll make some firm plans. Okay?'

The last thing Nic was aware of before he turned to the canvas was the beautiful smile on Gia's face. He lost himself in his work for the first time in a long time.

Chapter Fourteen

'Nic?'

Gia's voice interrupted Nic at the same time he noticed the rosy glow to the east. As he watched, a golden ray of light split the cloud and the rising sun broke the horizon. A fine strand of cobweb linking two scarlet geraniums shone in the soft golden light.

'Nic?' This time Gia's voice was louder and Nic put down his brush, rubbing his eyes before he turned around. Talking to Gia about what art meant to him last night—was it really morning already—had released something inside him. The hours had passed silently as each of them had been immersed in their own work. God knows how much longer he would have worked if she hadn't said his name. But even as he'd painted, his mind had been working and he'd made a plan for her exhibition. All he had to do was make some calls today to set it in motion. It was as easy as that. His thoughts turned to his painting as he'd worked. It was her passion and that passion spilled over to the bedroom.

He knew now he didn't hold that passion for art. Yes, he loved it, and he needed to be of the art world, but he was not consumed by it like Gia. Being on the Board of Trustees for the gallery would fill that need.

Why do I still paint? After spending time with Gia, and how she was driven, he suspected it was really more to do with that promise to his mother. As much as he'd dreamed of leaving the family business, Nic knew his passion was not enough to sustain life as an artist. He was an organiser who was lucky to be gifted with some talent.

Art doesn't drive me. Not like he'd seen it drive Gia as he'd watched her work.

Nic yawned, stretched and slowly turned around. He barely remembered taking his shirt off in the early hours as he'd become immersed in his painting. He grinned as Gia's face filled his vision. Scarlet, golden yellow, and a long slash of cobalt blue paint covered the right side of her face where she'd obviously been pushing her hair back. He dropped his gaze lower; her cropped T-shirt was covered with paint and he let his eyes linger on the outline of her breasts beneath the thin cotton.

'You look like one of the characters from *Avatar*.'

***

Gia's heart raced as Nic slowly walked across the room to her. Her mouth had dried as he'd lifted his arms and stretched, his muscles rippling across his back. When he turned around, her breath caught. A broad chest, lightly dusted with dark hair, with a tattooed word across the centre, took her mind far away from the work she had been engrossed in all night.

'Avatar? What do you mean?' She frowned as he slowly came closer, trying to keep calm but the thudding of her heart was filling her ears.

'The movie.' Nic reached up and brushed his fingers down the side of her face. And a grin lifted his lips. 'The one where their faces are blue. But yours is blue and yellow and scarlet.'

Gia laughed and reached to the workbench for a rag. 'So, I'm a messy artist. That is not new to me. But look at you.' She was having trouble keeping her eyes off Nic's bare—but clean—chest. 'How on earth do you paint without getting covered in paint?' Gia kept her face straight as an idea flitted through her head. 'Look, even your hands are clean.' She shook her head sadly and let out a fake sigh. 'Not a real artist. Nic.'

Nic's smile was teasing. 'I guess my technique is a tad superior to yours.'

She turned casually and picked up her paintbrush which was loaded with the last of the blue paint. 'Oh, I don't know about that. Let me help you.' Before he could guess her intention, she lunged at him with a laugh and painted a splotch of bright blue on his cheek. 'Now you look like a professional.'

Nic reached for the hand she held the brush in, but Gia was ready for him and slipped beneath his arm. She ran around to the other side of the workbench as laughter spilled over. 'I'm sorry. I just couldn't resist. You are a blank canvas waiting to be painted.'

Nic's eyes narrowed as he picked up another brush from the table and dipped it into her signature scarlet paint. 'You are so going to pay for that.'

Gia widened her eyes and took a step backward. She waited until Nic was almost close enough to reach her before she ducked down and crawled beneath the table, coming up on the other side with a triumphant cry.

'A bit slow, Nic? You'll never catch me.'

His eyes danced with mirth and Gia grinned back at him.

'We'll see about that. If you think you are going to get away with that, you, my lady, are in for a big shock.' Nic put one hand on the sturdy bench ready to jump over it. 'You think you know macho? I don't like to lose, Gia . . . in fact, I *always* win.'

Gia threw the brush down so she could make a quick getaway. Keeping Nic and the paintbrush he held in her sights, she backed toward her bedroom where there was a shower in a tiny ensuite bathroom. If she could just get to the door . . . she turned and ran.

'Not so fast, madam.' Nic dived around the edge of the bench and Gia ran toward the bedroom door with a shriek.

She almost made it but Nic's hand descended on her

shoulder before she could turn the handle. He twirled her around and kept his hand firmly on her arm as she stared up at him and the paintbrush he held above her head. His dark blue eyes were alight with laughter and Gia couldn't help the giggle that spilled from her lips. Life had been too serious for way too long. A warm rush of happiness flooded through her as she stared at his hand poised above her.

When did the joy of living disappear from my life? There was more to life than immersing herself in her art.

Gia avoided Nic's gaze and kept her eyes fixed firmly on the brush as it slowly inched closer and closer to her face. Her stomach fluttered—those damned butterflies had swooped back in, and she forced herself to stay still.

'*Hmm.* Let me see. Can I find a spot that needs attention?' Nic's voice was low and he was so close to her it vibrated through her skin. Gia looked down at his chest and her eyes lingered on the beautiful script that was embedded into his skin.

Corragio.

'The tattoo? Courage, Nic?' She grinned up at him 'I have no doubt you have plenty of that.'

Slowly he lowered the brush and for a moment, Gia thought she'd escaped retaliation for daubing his cheek with paint.

'Maybe you need a little courage, do you think, *bella*?'

He grabbed both of her hands with one of his and held the brush high with the other. Her breath caught as Nic used his body to gently push her back against the wall. She watched fascinated as he lowered his head and caught the thin straps of her T-shirt in his teeth and the stubble of his chin brushed her shoulder as he slid the strap down. A shaft of pure desire ran from her shoulder and honed straight between her legs. If Nic hadn't been supporting her with his body, Gia would have slid down the wall into a useless heap; her legs were trembling with anticipation.

She swallowed and lowered her voice. 'Courage for what?'

Nic lifted his head and held her gaze. 'To have faith in yourself and your exhibition. His eyes were half-closed but Gia watched with fascination as he leaned back and lowered the brush. The first strokes on the top of her breast were feather-soft and she tipped her head back and closed her eyes. A half swirl for the C and her fingers tingled with the need to touch Nic, but he still held her hands firmly in one of his. His brow was creased with concentration as his eyes remained firmly fixed on her breasts as the brush tickled her. The circle for the O was painstakingly slow and she was sure he was deliberately taking his time to complete each letter. The R was completed just as slowly and Gia closed her eyes when Nic began the next letter. The paint was cool on her skin and the sensation of the tip of the fine brush was sending quivers to her belly.

'*Hmmm*. We have a problem.'

Gia opened her eyes and smiled as she met Nic's intent stare. 'You've run out of paint?' she asked, not sure if she was pleased or disappointed.

'No, your T-shirt is in the way of the bottom of the two Gs.' Nic's grin was pure fun. 'I need to do this properly.'

'So, what will we do?' Gia ran her tongue along her top lip as she looked at Nic's bare chest in front of her. Sure, enough each G had a long tail that curled around like a crab claw. She took great satisfaction in his soft groan as he looked at her mouth.

'I can't lift your shirt over your head because the paint is still wet. That would ruin my fine work.' His voice was husky. 'If I let your hands go, can I trust you not to run away?'

'I'd hate for you not to finish the job you've started. An artist always completes their work. That is something I know.' Gia's voice was just as low and husky as Nic's. 'Perhaps you let me go and I'll slip the straps over my shoulders and pull my shirt down?'

Nic nodded and leaned back, holding the brush high as Gia's eyes locked with his. He placed his other hand on the wall beside her head. She smiled as she slipped first one, and then the other strap down over her shoulders before she held the bottom of her short T-shirt with her fingers. Gently she tugged it down until it began to slip over her skin. Nic's eyes bored into hers as the soft fabric slipped lower and lower, slowly revealing her bare breasts. He held her eyes with his and didn't look down until the soft cotton was pooled around her waist. Only then, did he drop his gaze and Gia straightened her shoulders as Nic's sigh washed over her.

'Much better.' This time he let her hands stay loose and Gia clenched her fists as Nic ran the brush down her right breast, slowly and gently in a long curl until it reached the tip of her nipple.

Gia had never experienced anything as erotic as the feel of the wet sable brush as it circled the aureole of her breast. A touch as soft as a feather as he formed the letter, Nic's attention was solely on her and the movement of the brush. Gia's attention was fixed on his hand as the brush dipped lower. The final two letters were completed and Nic leaned back with a soft sigh of satisfaction.

'Beautiful work, if I do say so.' He put the brush down on the small table beside them and cool air rushed onto her skin as he moved his body away from hers. 'But I guess you can't see it, can you?'

Gia shook her head wordlessly. Her skin was hypersensitive to Nic's touch and she shivered as he cupped his hand around the back of her neck and pulled her closer to him. The warmth of his hand travelled down her back and swirled around until it burst into heat that radiated throughout her entire body. She caught her breath as his lips came closer to hers and finally took her mouth. His other hand was still on the wall beside her and he didn't touch her anywhere else. Only his mouth touched hers, leaving Gia a quivering mess as his tongue danced with hers. Finally, he placed a last lingering kiss on her mouth and drew back, his breath brushing her still-sensitive lips as he spoke.

'Do you have a mirror?'

'In my bedroom.'

***

Nic had held himself back from the minute Gia had interrupted him while he was painting. The instant he had turned around and seen her, desire had flared through him. Her nipples had stood out through her thin T-shirt and her softly parted lips were open invitingly. But most enticing had been her playfulness when she had teased him. The game he had punished her with had been more a punishment for him—painting her breast slowly when all he wanted to do was drop his head and take her breast between his lips had been torture.

Now he looked down at her. Her expression was bemused, and he was tempted to kiss her again but he leaned back and he held out his hand.

'Take me there and you can see.' Nic looked down as Gia put her paint-stained hand trustingly in his. 'Please.'

Silently she led him into the bedroom and he drank in the curves of her slender bare back. She'd dropped the T-shirt and stepped out of it in the studio. Her skin was flawless and the curve of her back as it reached her waist, enticing. He forced his gaze away from the sexy indentations at the base of her spine. He looked up and met her eyes in the mirror. Both of them were as dark-haired as the other, but while Nic's hair was in a neat shortcut, as usual, Gia's was in a wild cloud around her head. Nic's mouth dried as he stood behind her and watched as she lifted her hand and slowly traced her fingers over the now-dry paint on her breast.

'*Corragio*,' she whispered. 'Yes, I will have courage.'

Nic lowered his head and placed his lips on Gia's neck and she trembled against him as he tasted her sweet skin. With a groan, he lifted his head slightly and murmured against her ear. 'What do you want to do now? Do you need to sleep?' Gia leaned back against him and her bare skin rubbed against his chest. She arched her neck and reached back, lifting his hands and placing them on her breasts. 'No.'

Nic needed no more invitation. He half-turned her before lifting her in his arms. The bed was unmade, the blankets pulled back and hanging over to one side. He pushed them aside with his leg and lowered Gia gently onto the bed. Her hair spread out on the white lace pillowcase in a black tangle, contrasting with the smudges of paint on her face. Her lips parted softly in a sexy, inviting smile.

Never before had he felt such a deep desire to claim a woman as his own. He stood beside the bed and looked down at the beautiful woman lying in front of him. No artifice, no care about how she looked. Her hair was wild, paint covered one side of her face—Nic smiled—and the word on her breasts marked her as his. It was a shame it would wash off.

***

Gia knew that Nic was a generous lover. It was in the way he moved, and in the way he held her gaze as though he knew what she wanted. Now it was her turn to be generous. She lay back on the pillow and opened her arms to him. Nic's mouth met hers as their lips joined. He moved slowly, teasing her. When he lifted his head, Gia turned hers from side to side, her chest heaving as she gasped in deep breaths. His bare skin against hers, his heat deep inside her, sent waves of exquisite pleasure rolling over her and she stared back into his deep blue eyes.

Chapter Fifteen

Bright sunlight shining on his face woke Nic with a start. The sun was high in the sky and he looked around but there was no clock in the room. Gia's legs were entangled with his and she slept beside him, breathing softly through slightly parted lips. Nic lay there for a moment looking at her. Her black hair was spread on the pillow and her cheeks held a soft rosy flush. The white pillowcase was now a myriad of colours from her cheek. Just looking at her sent another surge of desire running rampant through his blood. He rolled away carefully, and Gia slept on without stirring. Nic lay back, put his hands behind his head and stared at the ceiling, wondering what the hell had hit him.

Two days—only two days— and this beautiful woman had him under her spell and that worried him. This loss of self-control was unfamiliar to him. He couldn't figure Gia out. She was an enigma. Not like any other woman he had ever met. One minute she was shy and her lack of conviction frustrated him— the next, her vitality surfaced and she went for what she wanted with a ferocity that amazed him. From an innocent with her head bent down, to a confident woman with a wit that made him laugh. And a touch that had given him pleasure for hours until she'd fallen asleep in his arms.

Before they'd ended up in bed, as he'd painted all night with her in the studio, he'd been aware of her on one level but immersed in creating the best piece he had ever painted, as she'd worked silently across the room from him. Her passion had flared and she'd responded to him as *Nic*, not because of who he was or what he had. Her attraction to him had nothing to do with the Baldini name and that pleased him. The problem was, how was he going to handle it? He needed to set things up so he could leave when the time came. No regrets, no ties, and no one who had a hold on him or his heart. He would never put himself in that vulnerable position. His life plan was mapped out, and there was no place in it for a passionate black-haired artist with flashing eyes. When she found out he was a Baldini, and that his discovery of her talent and launching her into the Florentine art world had secured—God he hoped he was right—his position on the Board, he had a feeling that the true Gia, that strong passionate woman, would have plenty more to say.

The guilt that settled in his chest was unfamiliar, but he pushed it away when his phone vibrated. He eased out of bed so he didn't wake Gia, and searched for his phone, finding it in his jeans on the floor.

He frowned. Five missed calls from Antonio and two from his father.

##

Nic went back to the villa for a change of clothes, and he had time for a quick coffee before he'd head for the *autostrada* to Florence. He looked around the villa. Even though it was luxurious, and decorated in bright colours, it was empty . . . soulless. Gia's old stone cottage was full of life and colour. Noise and vibrancy. He grinned as he imagined her walking in here. This place would come alive. He'd take down the paintings and line the entry walls with her landscapes…

Whoa, I'm on holidays and I have a problem that needs dealing with.

Nic shook his head and forced his thoughts to the problem at hand. Antonio had been furious on the phone, and Nic had calmed him.

'I'm on my way.'

The manager of one of his charities had taken ill, and when Antonio had been looking at the accounts, he had noticed a significant discrepancy. The trusted manager had been siphoning funds into his own account, and if he hadn't taken ill, it would have been months before the fraud would have come to light.

And not only that, Antonio told him he'd heard a whisper that the announcement of the new Board member might be decided sooner, and that set Nic's planning for Gia's exhibition into overdrive. He switched his phone to hands-free and called

Ben, his PA, and within an hour and before he had crossed the *Ponte alla Carraia* to the city, most of the logistics had been decided. Ben was on it and the invitations would go out tonight. First ones to the trustees of the Uffizi. A simple parchment invitation with gold writing . . . with no hint about Gia or her paintings. Only her name, as an enticement.

Nic Baldini presents Gia Carelli.

God, he'd have to make sure she didn't see any of them until the show was over. Nic knew that his name as the organiser would guarantee attendance by the elite and the critics. Discovering Gia and introducing her to the art world of the city would guarantee his position.

Antonio took a step back and stared at Nic when he pushed open the door of his Florence office. Nic took a deep breath as the familiar thrill ran through him. Narrowing his eyes, he glanced up at the screen in the corner that was always tuned in to the stock market and nodded with satisfaction as the figures flashed across the screen.

Good. The Baldini stocks were performing well. He grinned ruefully.

And had continued to do so without me watching constantly. I haven't looked at the market for forty-eight hours. Maybe Mamma's idea of there being more to life than work had something to it.

'My God, look at you. I'll have to go to Tuscany for a holiday. How long have you been there?' Antonio shook his head. 'You look like you're already rested and ready to take the business world by storm.'

'Just a couple of days.' Nic grinned at his little brother. He wasn't about to share how amazing those days had been.

'What have you been doing? Found a golf course?'

Nic shook his head. Antonio thought he'd gone there to look at the renovations. 'Just . . . sampling the local delicacies.'

Oh, yes.

'How's your villa look?'

'Fantastic. The builders did a great job. And you should see the decor.' Nic was pleased Antonio had changed the subject. He wanted to tell him all about Gia, and how wonderful she was, but not yet. 'It's ready for the first group of artists in a couple of weeks.'

Antonio grinned at him and squeezed his shoulder in a rare show of brotherly affection. 'You're a good man, Nic. Mamma would have been pleased with what you did with your share of her trust fund. She always said you were the benevolent one.'

Nic grinned back at his brother. 'Do you remember that time she took us down to that village? I've been thinking about it these past few days.'

Antonio frowned and shook his head. 'Not sure. Which time? She was always taking us on an adventure somewhere. It's a wonder either of us ever got an education. Which village do you mean?'

'The one where I got my tattoo.' Nic tapped his chest.

'Oh yes, that was the first time I'd ever seen a real gypsy.' Antonio laughed. 'I was expecting a caravan in the middle of a field, but she was quite a well-groomed woman in an old villa. She read my palm, too.'

'I never forgot my reading. I don't know if it was the impetus that gave me the idea for starting up the artist's retreat, or whether she was a fortune teller who really could predict the future. But she'd said I'd be involved in charities.'

Nic frowned as Antonio stared over his shoulder and muttered. 'I hope it was a coincidence, not that I believe in that mumbo jumbo shit, anyway.'

'Why, what did she say to you?'

Antonio shrugged. 'She told me that I wouldn't be happy until I had experienced a tragedy in my life.'

'Pretty crap thing to say to a teenager.'

'Yeah, but I didn't let it bother me.'

Nic narrowed his eyes. 'Doesn't look like it. You're still talking about it.'

'Come on, we've got work to do. Unless you're not going

back to the villa? I bet you've had enough vacation already, I'd say, knowing you, Mr Workaholic. Keen to get back to work? Here to stay?'

Nic crossed to the desk. 'Oh, I'm going back. I might even extend my month for the rest of the summer if we sort this mess out quickly.'

'Ha ha, bro. Pull the other one.' Antonio's brow wrinkled as he picked up the file from the desk. 'Knowing you, you're working from the office at the villa.'

Nic simply smiled. He knew he was detail-oriented—and controlling— when it came to his charity work and the marble business, and it blew him away that he hadn't really given either of them a thought until Antonio had called him. All of his energy had gone into launching Gia.

And being in her bed.

Hell, if he didn't get her out of his head, they'd never sort this mess out this afternoon; he wanted to go back to Castellina.

'Did you get any other calls?' Antonio glanced at him curiously as he pulled up a report on the large computer screen on Nic's desk, and Nic leaned forward, running his finger down the screen.

'There were some missed calls from our father.' He stopped at a large transaction on the screen. 'I see what you mean.'

'So, did he tell you he's coming over to the office?'

'No, I didn't return his call. I'm on holidays, remember?'

'Jesus, Nic. I don't know what it is with you and Papa. Can't you make an effort?'

Nic swung around to face his brother. 'An effort? Why should I? Ever since Mamma died, he's treated me as though I don't exist, unless it's to criticise something I've done.'

Antonio stared at him. 'You're too hard on him. It's a two-way street.'

'That's bullshit and you know it. The only reason he'll be coming over now is to gloat because one of *my* projects is in trouble. He's totally lost interest in the business, but anything that makes me look bad, he'll be straight here.'

'You know why, don't you? It's because you are so much like Mamma. You have the same eyes and the same way of seeing things. I see the way he looks at you when you are not watching. His grief is still tearing him apart.'

Nic let out a bitter laugh. 'Grief? He never even mentions her.'

'Not to you, maybe. I think he finds it hard to talk to you because you are the image of Mamma.' Antonio shook his head thoughtfully. 'And I don't need a gypsy fortune teller to explain why you work so hard. You've been trying to prove yourself to Papa ever since he wouldn't let you go to the Academy.' He lowered his voice. 'And to yourself.'

Nic ignored his brother's words. 'Show me what you've found.'

They spent a couple of hours going over the online transactions, and their father arrived just as they were winding up. Being such a high-profile company meant the bank would take a call from the Baldinis any time of the day or night, especially when the call was made by the senior Baldini.

'Nic.' Their father nodded briefly and then ignored his eldest son as he made the call.

'Have you called the police?' Nic frowned at Antonio as he scanned the transactions. 'It's not a huge amount, but it's still fraudulent.'

'Do you know Livio's story?' His father spoke as he ended the call and helped himself to a coffee from Nic's coffee maker.

'No, I've lost touch with the staff here in Florence since I took over at Carrara. Why?'

'His youngest son has cancer, and he took the money to help with the medical costs.'

Nic lifted his head from the screen and stared at his father. 'You're joking? Why the fuck didn't he come to us for help?'

'He was scared you'd refuse to help him.'

Nic shook his head in disbelief. 'Of course, I would've

helped him out. Livio has been a loyal employee for a long time. That's why I found this so hard to believe.'

His father stared back at him. 'He sees you as a hard businessman. Like everyone does. He wouldn't even have considered that you would listen.'

Nic slammed his hand down on the desk. 'That's bullshit and you know it.' Hell, he donated *millions* to children's hospitals.

'Is it, Nic?' His father's eyes were fixed on him.

'Yes, it is. But it doesn't matter. Maybe I won't be a part of all this crap soon. I'm thinking of changing direction. I'll leave it to Antonio to look after the export contracts.'

'And what are you going to do?' His father's gaze didn't waver from his. He hadn't noticed before how deep the wrinkles had become around his father's eyes.

Antonio stood between them as father and son eyeballed each other. Always the peacemaker. 'Like I said before, Nic. You're a good man. It's in your nature to help people out. We know that. A lot of people wouldn't expect that. They just see the businessman who works so hard.'

'Set up an appointment with him next week. I'll be away again. I'll Zoom.'

'And the police?'

Nic waved his hand dismissively. 'No, of course not. We

won't press charges.' He managed to keep the conversation civil before he left, but Antonio's words stayed in his head.

They just see the businessman who works so hard. The words went around and around in his head. The thought that Livio would rather steal than ask him for help made him sick to the stomach.

Gia didn't see him like that. Nic frowned as he turned off the freeway heading for Castellina. Maybe was about time he told her who he was. Once he got the show organised, he would come clean. Then once he got the position on the board he would decide if he needed Baldini Enterprises. He didn't need the money. Maybe he didn't need to be part of the family business. Maybe he didn't need to be part of the Baldini family, either. He didn't need his father

His chest closed with anger—and guilt— as he sped through the valleys.

Chapter Sixteen

Gia woke to an empty bed in the early afternoon. It was Sunday and she didn't have to work tonight—the one night she had at home. She sat up and pushed her hair back from her face. Slipping from the bed, she put on her spectacles and grimaced when she saw the state of her grandmother's lace pillowcases. She grabbed the white silk robe that always hung over the bedpost. There was no sign of Nic in the studio but the painting he had worked on was still there. Gia smiled; he was getting to know her well. A note was stuck to the side of the easel. Nic must have known this was the first place she would go to.

Gone to the villa. Call me when you wake up. I have a show to organise. His writing, and the mobile number which followed the message, were written in a beautiful scrolling script just like the tattoo on his chest. Gia drew a quick breath as she remembered how he had painted the same word on her breasts this morning. She looked down; it was still there.

Moving her eyes back to the easel, she took a step back and let out a soft gasp as she looked at the picture in front of her. Mauve moonlight bathed her courtyard in a wash of gentle colour, and she sat on a chair beside a garden. Nic had painted her face in shadow with no expression apparent. Her body was relaxed, and he had clothed her in a white peasant dress, innocent, yet sexy, as it dropped off her shoulder. He had painted her skin glowing in the moonlight. It was a gorgeous country scene. Serene, peaceful, and beautiful. It was full of *him*. His calm nature spoke to her from the canvas. His style was very different from hers, soft colours, where hers were harsh and strident, precise and considered strokes where hers were bold. It was a controlled creation. She grinned, very much like his character.

But he is good . . . very, very good.

Looking at his work was like looking at Nic. Sensual, instinctive, and romantic; never in her life had she met anyone like him. He wore the independence she so desperately sought like a second skin. He was confident and knew what he wanted, and went for it. He was a planner and every part of his life seemed to be under control.

How good would that be?

To seek adventure and excitement away from home; her dreams could be fulfilled if Nic's offer to help her with an exhibition came to fruition. It was a testament to his generous nature and Gia sensed that was a big part of who he was. Maybe it was wishful thinking that she was seeing it in his painting as well. But Nic was kind and generous—what she saw was the real Nic, she had no doubt of that. She had trusted him enough to let her guard down and be herself. She would miss him when he left.

Gia was thoughtful as she headed for the shower. She paused in front of the mirror where Nic had held her last night. Slowly she traced the fingers over the reversed letters before letting out a soft sigh and stepping beneath the hot water. She had a lot of work to do if she was going to have an exhibition. She could not waste a single moment.

After Gia had showered and stripped the paint-stained bed, she called Nic but he didn't pick up. A little disappointed, she ignored the little tug of doubt that ran through her and turned back to the painting she'd been working on last night. If he hadn't wanted her to call him, he wouldn't have left his cell number. Soon, she forgot her worries and was immersed in her world of colour.

Hunger stirred her hours later, and she broke from her work as the light began to fade. Gia crossed the room and pulled the old-fashioned cord that turned the light on. She stood and looked at the room with a critical eye. Nic seemed certain that it was a suitable venue for a show but she wasn't sure. The few times she'd been to exhibitions in galleries in Florence, the setting had been slick and sophisticated. Not a room with crooked stone walls and poor lighting not to mention faulty plumbing. She could just imagine some of the art aficionados she had observed in Florence looking for the ladies' restroom.

Uncertainty hit hard.

No. Gia shook her head with a frown. It just wouldn't work. Nic's boyish enthusiasm had sucked her in and she hadn't thought it through. They'd signed no agreement, so she could change her mind. Now that she was away from his enthusiasm—and he had to admit his decision-making—she was having second thoughts. They would talk when he came back.

Her life would go back to normal after his holiday; she would just enjoy being with him while he was here. He said he had an apartment in Florence; maybe they could stay in touch when he went back to work. His enthusiasm to help her out and have a show had blinded him to the difficulties of holding it. She shrugged and opened the pantry in her small kitchen. It was almost bare; there'd been no time to restock. When she thought of shopping it was usually the middle of the night and the local store was closed. And as she told Nic, she hated cooking.

Oh well, Papa will be pleased. She was going to have to wander down the hill for dinner. She had tried Nic's phone a couple more times but he hadn't answered and it hadn't gone to voicemail, which was strange. Gia shrugged as she changed into warmer clothes to walk down to *Giannino's*. He'd turn up when he was good and ready. She wouldn't stress but she couldn't resist trying one more time as she pulled the door shut behind her.

'Nic Ba—' His deep voice answered on the first ring, and there was silence. Gia sensed that Nic cut off the rest of his greeting. For a moment she even thought the call had been disconnected.

'Nic?'

'Gia . . . sorry I had to pull the car over.'

'Where are you?'

Nic's voice faded in and out; it wasn't a good connection. 'I had to take a trip to Florence . . . had a call . . . on the way back now.'

'I tried to call you earlier.' For some reason she needed him to know that, and then she was cross with herself for being so transparent.

'I'm on my way back now. Are you working tonight?'

'No. But I was just about to head down for dinner.' Gia looked out over the hills. A storm was sweeping up the valley; the tops of the hills were wreathed in mist. She would have to go back inside for her umbrella.

'Can you wait half an hour for me? How about I take you somewhere different?'

Happiness filled her. She hadn't been confident enough to admit to herself that deep down she had wondered if Nic would come back or not. 'Yes. I'll wait at my cottage.'

Gia disconnected and gave in to vanity. She ran into her

bedroom and tugged off the old jeans and paint-stained shirt she had been going to wear to the family restaurant. Eating in the kitchen at *Giannino's* didn't require dress clothes, even though it would have gotten a frown from Gabriel. She stood in front of her meagre wardrobe, flicking through old shirts and baggy skirts. Over the past few months, her clothes had become looser. She'd worked harder than ever to save enough money to move to Florence. Gia knew she didn't eat properly but the last thing she felt like doing was eating at the end of a long shift. Riding her bike, running around the restaurant, up and down the stairs, and through the courtyard kept her fit.

She settled on a dress she had bought on a whim. It had reminded her of one of her paintings. It was like the dress she had worn out to lunch with Nic but it was lower cut at the front.

Gia grinned as she slipped it over her head and crossed to the mirror, nodding with satisfaction as her reflection confirmed what she'd hoped for.

The top of the words that Nic had painted on her breast were clearly visible above the low neckline of her dress. She'd taken a very careful shower earlier, not wanting it to wash off, although it would probably take a good scrubbing with turpentine to remove the word. She was well used to that; it was a wonder the skin on her face wasn't wrinkled like an old canvas. It received a daily dose of turpentine to remove the paint stains each night before she headed to work. Gabriel could barely cope with her paint-stained fingers, if she turned up with paint on her face, he would go ballistic.

Gia's smile grew as she wondered what her family would think of her pseudo-tattoo. She fluffed out her hair with her fingers, removed her spectacles, slipped in her contacts and settled down to wait for Nic. It was the happiest she had been in a long time, and although it felt good, confusion filled her.

Is it because he values my work? And wants to show it? Or is it because the chance of escaping to the city is almost within reach?

But the image that came to mind as she stared at the landscapes propped against the wall was of a dimpled chin and full, sexy lips.

***

Nic drew a quick breath when Gia pushed the gate open as he pulled up in the Roadster. Her dress was a bright slash of colourful flowers. Huge red poppies dotted a yellow background. It hugged her breasts and was nipped in at the waist before flaring out just above her knees. Long, bare legs were the first thing Nic saw as he climbed out of the car and met her at the gate.

'Hello, Sleeping Beauty. I didn't have the heart to wake you when I left.' He lowered his head and captured her lips with his, warmth filling him as she pressed her body against his and her lips opened beneath his mouth.

'Kiss me like that some more and we won't get to dinner.' Her voice was low and throaty against his lips, and Nic closed his eyes, giving himself into the warmth of her skin.

'Where is my shy little waitress? The temptress is back.' He was tempted to take Gia back inside, but then he looked at her. Her eyes were highlighted with a grey shadow, and her lips were painted deep scarlet to match the poppies on her dress. She'd dressed up for dinner. He'd take her out.

He put his hand up to his mouth. 'Uh-oh. Am I wearing lipstick now?'

Gia grinned and shook her head. 'One of my few extravagances. It doesn't come off.'

'Good.' Nic dipped his head and kissed her again. When he pulled back his eyes dropped to her chest and he smiled. The soft swell of her breasts peeked out above the low neckline of her dress. The top of the word he had painted there rose above the brightly-coloured fabric.

Coraggio. Still emblazoned on her breast.

'*Hmm.* The lipstick is obviously as good a quality as the paint I used. It hasn't come off either.' Nic held Gia's chin gently and turned her head from side to side, pretending to examine her closely. 'The blue cheeks are gone, which is a plus. Not sure if the fancy restaurant would like that look.'

Gia turned to the car and opened the door. 'Take me there. I'm starving.' She looked at him from beneath her eyelashes. 'If I'm presentable enough?'

'Are you fishing for compliments? You look stunning. I'd like to call into your family restaurant. I don't think they'd recognise their gorgeous, confident daughter.'

'Uh-uh.' Gia shook her head with a laugh and pointed to her breast. 'Do you want to be shot at dawn?'

The restaurant Nic took Gia to was tucked into the corner of the fortified wall that surrounded the village and looked down over the western valley. Word would soon get back to her family that she was out with Nic Battistoni. When they were seated at the table on the high terrace overlooking the olive groves to the west, Nic ordered a bottle of champagne.

Gia narrowed her eyes. '*Dom Perignon*? Do you know how expensive that is?'

Nic laughed and nodded at the waiter. 'Two glasses, please.' He took Gia's hand and held it on the snow-white linen tablecloth. 'Yes, I do. But this is a celebration.'

Gia tipped her head to the side. 'A celebration?'

Nic shook his head and waited till the waiter returned. The man fussed with the bottle before he paused, looking at Gia, his eyes wide. 'Gia?'

'Hello, Stefano. I didn't realise you were working here. What happened to your work at the olive grove? I thought you'd been promoted to manager.'

The waiter shot a quick glance at Nic and their joined hands on the table. He shrugged. 'Second job. Caro's having another baby and can't work.'

'Number three?'

Stefano shook his head. 'Number four.'

'Well, congratulations. And pass my best wishes to Caro.'

Stefano stood there looking at Gia with a wistful look on his face. Nic cleared his throat and the man jumped, and then he popped the champagne and filled their glasses before going back to the bar.

'What was all that about? That guy looked like he was about to cry when he recognised you.'

Nic watched Gia as her face coloured. 'Old boyfriend. Papa was disappointed when I broke it off with him. She shuddered. '*Ergh*. What a lucky escape. Caro's younger than me and she's having baby number *four*.'

Nic smiled as she shivered.

'So back to our celebration.' He let go of Gia's hand and picked up his glass and waited for her to pick up hers. 'A toast to you'—he smiled at her and a rush of feeling buzzed through him as she smiled back— 'the up-and-coming new artist, the mysterious Gia Carelli will be having her first exhibition three weeks from today.'

'Three weeks? Gia put her glass down and her eyes widened. 'From today? Oh, Nic. I can't be ready in three weeks. And besides I've been having second thoughts since you left.'

'Why not? Give me one good reason.' He sat back and watched her deflate in front of him.

'The studio's a mess.'

'I'll help you clean it up.'

She shook her head. 'The catering. There's no way that can be organised in time.'

'All done. Next?'

'Um . . .'

Nic lowered his gaze to the soft swell of her breast peeking above the neckline of her dress. 'How about you look down at the single word gracing your beautiful skin?'

Gia dropped her eyes too, and Nic was pleased to see a slow smile spread across her face.

'Now tell me. What does it say? '

'It says *coraggio*,' Her smile got wider but then Nic frowned as Gia pushed her chair back and it scraped on the tiled floor.

'I can do it.' She came around to his side of the table and leaned down and planted a smacking kiss on his cheek. 'I *can* do it!'

Her excitement was infectious and Nic grabbed her hand and lifted her fingers to his mouth. 'Of course, you can, and it is going to set your career on a stellar path. You keep producing beautiful work and you will soon be known all over Europe.'

Gia moved back to her chair and Nic thought if eyes could sparkle, hers would rival the stars he had painted her beneath last night.

'I'm having an exhibition!' She hugged her arms as she held his gaze. 'Gia Carelli from Castellina is an artist!'

'Of course, you are. You always have been. Having an exhibition doesn't change that.' Nic put a serious note into his voice. 'Have you ever thought about a business manager?'

'What? No. Why would I need one of them?'

'Because, my sweet, I predict you are going to make a lot of money.'

'Enough to move to Florence?'

'Probably enough to move to Paris, or Rome or New York . . . wherever the mood takes you.'

Gia sat across the table from him and shook her head. Disbelief was written all over her face. A surge of affection— *that's all it is*—ran through Nic. It was the same—but sort of different—to the feeling he got when he helped out the sick children. This was more personal and he wondered what it meant. Maybe, if—when—she moved to Florence, they could spend some time together. But he had a feeling that she was about to leave him far behind in the art world. *No, it didn't matter.*

He didn't want a close connection with anyone. He would enjoy letting Gia go and watching her fly.

That's how much I believe in her.

'Nic? Nic?'

Nic stared at Gia and realised she had been talking to him. 'Sorry, I was dreaming of your stellar career.'

'I know you're busy with your work and everything . . . and your painting, but I was wondering if—' she looked away— 'you would be my business manager?'

Nic could see her confidence fading fast. Regret filled him as her voice trailed off and he shook his head slowly. 'I hope I haven't overstepped the mark, but I've already made a call and asked someone I know—through my work—if they'd talk to you. It's not the sort of thing I do.'

Nic had no doubt he could do it with his eyes shut, but Gia deserved the attention of someone who could give her more time than he could. Ben was not only one of his most trusted staff, but a good friend. He would set her in the right direction and help her to liaise with the right people. Nic didn't want to tell her that although he was based in Carrara, he frequently travelled back and forth to the States.

Not yet. And maybe not for much longer anyway. His gut burned as he thought of the argument with his father this afternoon, and he picked up his glass and let the cool wine soothe his throat.

He could have told her who he was, but he wasn't going to. Not yet. When it was all done. He didn't want to put the next weeks he had left with her at risk.

He wanted Gia to feel that she had achieved this with the quality of her work, and not because of the Baldini name behind the show.

I'll tell her later. When it's all done.

Her face coloured and she mumbled softly. 'Sorry, I know it was a lot to ask of you.'

Nic reached over the table and took her hand in his. Her nails were short and it appeared no matter how much she scrubbed them, there was always a rim of coloured paint on the side of her fingers.

'No, Gia. It's not because of that. It's because you need someone who can give you the right advice and spend time on your career.' He wrinkled his brow. 'I might have to go back to work a little earlier than I planned, and I wouldn't have enough time to help you properly. Like you deserve. You have to realise that this show is going to put you up with the big players and you'll need a plan.'

She opened her mouth but he interrupted her before she could speak. 'But I'll be down here both weekends to help you get the studio ready. All you have to do is keep painting and then get glammed up on the day.'

Her smile was shy. 'If you're going to come down for the weekends . . . would you like . . . to save paying for somewhere to stay . . . it would make sense . . . if you stayed with me.'

Nic smiled. 'I'd love to take you up on that offer.' He let a devilish smile cross his face to cover the guilt that rippled through him. One day he'd show Gia the villa. Next time he came back. *If she's still here.* 'But on one condition.'

Gia frowned. 'What's that?'

'We can't spend all day and night in your bed. As much as I'd like to, we'll have to work hard.'

This time Gia's smile was wide as she tipped one finger to her lips. 'Oh, but we'll be tired after our hard work and I'm sure we'll have to go to bed sometime.'

'Speaking of which . . . maybe we should order and then we can go back to your place and see what needs to be done.' He moved his fingers slowly up and down the inside of her wrist. 'How long it's going to take to get the space ready . . . and how much time we'll have left to play.'

Nic turned and raised his hand to summon Stefano over

to take their order. He was eager to get home and do something about the way Gia was looking at him.

Chapter Seventeen

The next week passed quickly. It was the happiest Gia could ever remember being. For the first time, the emotion and the happiness that came from her painting spilled over into the rest of her life. She and Nic painted together; they walked, they slept—Gia smiled to herself—well, maybe not, but they did spend a lot of time in her bed. They laughed together. Nic moved his painting equipment over from the villa and spent the days and nights at her cottage. The only thing that niggled at her was how he had taken over—almost as though she needed looking after. She shook her head and dismissed her doubt. That was unfair. He didn't need to help her and he was doing so much to ensure her show would go off without a hitch. Her independence was still there. Seeing Stefano in the restaurant the other night had cemented her determination to get away from the village. Without Nic, there would be no exhibition.

If Nic could help her do that, she would take everything he offered. She loved being with him, he was great fun, he made her laugh and . . . the sex was amazing. Her stomach muscles gave a little tug just thinking about him.

He would leave, but she would have fun while he was here. Once she managed to put aside that feeling of being overwhelmed, and a little out of control, her happiness was complete. She worked at the restaurant each night, noticing many a curious look between her father and brother, but she put her head down and worked quietly.

Gabriel caught her arm one night as she hurried past him back to the kitchen. 'Gia, where are your spectacles? Don't you go tripping over in the kitchen because you can't see properly?'

She looked up at her brother and grinned. 'No need to worry, Gabe. I am wearing contacts.'

'And new clothes.' He looked at her thoughtfully and she smiled.

'Yes, new clothes.'

'Why?'

Gia pulled a face at him. Had she really been that bland, that by simply taking more notice of what she wore was noticed by her family? 'Why what?'

'Why do you suddenly seem so happy? You are . . . different.' He stared down at her and she held her brother's gaze steadily. 'I heard you were out the other night. You haven't taken on more than you can handle, have you?'

'More than I can handle?' She looked up at her brother and grinned. 'You mean, a man?'

'No, I mean Nic. He's a bit out of your league, isn't he?'

Hurt suffused her chest, and she bit back the angry retort

that sprang to her lips. 'Whatever you think.' She would not let her family take over her happiness. Pushing past her brother, she kept her head down as she walked toward the kitchen. 'I've got meals to take out.'

Finally, on Friday night, she summoned up the courage to mention Nic to her father. Although the village grapevine—and her brother—had probably filled him in on the details already.

It had been a busy night and the kitchen was chaotic. Gabriel had hired two extra girls from the village to work in the kitchen and Gia had run all night, taking orders, delivering meals, and clearing tables. Finally, the last guest paid their bill and Papa summoned Gabriel and Gia to the table beside the door.

'Come over here, my children. I think we all deserve a break. That is the biggest night we have had so far this summer.'

'Bodes well for the season.' Gabriel smiled.

Gia leaned back in the chair and looked into the courtyard as Papa lifted a bottle.

'Limóncello, Gia?'

She nodded. *Anything to help fortify my courage.*

'Just one though, you know how silly wine makes you.'

Mou Mou brushed the side of Gia's leg and she reached down and pulled the cat up onto her lap, trying not to pull a face at her father. She kept her head down and stroked the cat as Papa filled Gabriel's glass and then half-filled hers.

'To a successful season.' His loud voice boomed across the empty courtyard.

'Papa?' Gia spoke hesitantly. Mou-Mou stretched up and snuggled into her T-shirt and Gia focused on the cat, stroking the pet to calm her nerves.

'Yes, *bella.*?'

'I . . . I have met someone and I would like to bring him to lunch tomorrow. Would that be all right?'

'Of course, of course. That is wonderful to hear.' Papa's face split into a huge grin and his drooping moustache wobbled. 'He is not from the village?'

'It is Nic that bought my paintings. Nic Battistoni who is staying at the Baldini place.' Gabriel glanced at her sharply. She was tempted to poke her tongue at him; the look of disapproval on her brother's face was uncalled for. It was *none* of his business.

'He is from Florence. Well, for now, anyway.' Gia lifted her head. 'He works at Carrara, and he is going to help me—'

'So, he told you he *works* for the Baldinis?' Gabriel's stare was intent.

What is his problem?

'Gabriel, leave your sister alone. It is wonderful that she is seeing a young man.'

'But—'

'Enough.' Papa held his hand up at Gabriel and turned to her. 'That is all good. Any friend of yours is welcome at our table. He was a very nice gentleman. I will look forward to talking to him again.'

She took a deep breath and the cat jumped off her lap. That went well. While the going was good, she forged on. 'And Papa, there is something else I want to tell you.'

His eyes narrowed and Gia could see he was expecting to hear something he didn't like.

God, am I so transparent? She sat up straight in her chair, lifting her chin.

'Nic is helping me with my art.'

'Helping you? How? By buying your little pictures?' Papa shook his head. 'He paid too much for them, I think.'

Gabriel hadn't spoken and was looking from one to the other, following the conversation with interest. Her temper began to simmer and she fought it back, remembering the faith that Nic had in her work

Paris, Rome, New York, he'd said. And she trusted him.

'No, he is helping me set up a show of my work.'

Papa frowned. 'Why would he want to do that? Who would look at them?'

Support came from an unexpected quarter. 'Gia's work *is* okay, Papa.' Gabriel spoke slowly. 'It will be good for her.'

'*Pah.*' Papa dismissed her brother's words. 'She doesn't need that. What she needs is a husband and a home in the village. Forget all about this art nonsense.' He turned to Gia and patted her hand. 'You'll grow out of it, *bella,* and you'll find a husband soon. Don't you worry about that.'

Heat filled Gia's cheeks and she bit the side of her cheek to stop the angry words flowing. The last thing she was worried about was a husband, but she didn't want to create a scene, especially with Nic coming to the family lunch tomorrow.

Ignoring Papa, Gia reached out and lightly touched Gabriel's arm. 'Thank you.'

She was rewarded with an encouraging smile from her usually impatient brother.

***

Gia smoothed down the plain, white T-shirt she had put on with her jeans to wear to lunch at home. Her colourful clothes stayed in the cupboard. Being with Nic every day and night made her newfound confidence flourish. His faith in her work and the enjoyment he took in her company made her feel good about herself. But her self-confidence had taken a pummelling at the hands of her father last night.

She and Nic had slept in after a late night and he had gone back to the villa for the first time in a few days, to get some more clothes and to make some business calls. Gia wondered why he would be making business calls while he was on holidays but soon forgot about that in her nervousness. She was hesitant about taking Nic to meet the family, even though he'd already met Papa and Gabriel.

Walking across to the window she looked down the valley. It was a brilliant day and she expected that Mamma would have the table set up outside. The family home was on the other side of the village and overlooked the lavender fields. At least if they were outside, it wouldn't be so difficult if there was an awkward lull in the conversation. She grinned ruefully—there would be little fear of that with her noisy family.

Why am I so worried about the family liking Nic?

He would be gone soon, and their time together would be over. He'd hinted about seeing her when he went back to work, but Gia didn't let herself hope for one moment that he would really follow through when he left.

She gave herself a mental shake. He would still be here for the next two weekends and then for the show. She must trust him. Taking a deep breath, she let assurance fill her. If Nic said he would come, he would.

The low purr of his little sports car came up the winding road and Gia hurried across to the door, casting a longing look at her easel. She would much prefer to spend the afternoon painting with him but she couldn't miss two lunches in a row.

Mamma would have her moving back home and Gia couldn't think of anything she'd hate more.

A deep breath and she closed the door behind her as Nic vaulted the fence and hurried across the courtyard.

'There is a gate, you know.' Her voice was dry but she smiled at him. Nic had dressed up for the occasion. He wore a pale-blue collared shirt and dark jeans. Gia looked down at her plain clothes. She couldn't carry off flamboyant colours at a family lunch. She preferred to fade into the background. Mamma had called to let her know that the cousins were coming over from Montepulciano and she hoped it wasn't purely because she was bringing Nic to lunch.

This could be a very awkward afternoon.

Why the hell did I invite him?

'Yes,'—Nic caught her in his arms and planted a hard kiss on her mouth— 'but I like to impress a pretty woman.' He placed his finger beneath her chin and tipped her head up. 'What's with the frown and the black and white clothes? Where's my colourful Gia gone?'

'Oh, Nic, I am so nervous about this lunch.' He was such a kind and thoughtful guy. That's why she had invited him to come along. All would be well.

It would.

'Why? It's your family? Would you rather go alone? '

'Oh no. I want you to meet them and I want you to tell Papa all about the plans for my show. He was less than enthusiastic when I mentioned it . . . but you know what? For the first time in twenty-three years, Gabriel actually supported me. I nearly fainted.' She laughed. 'If I had, Papa would have blamed the Limóncello!

Nic frowned. 'Why?'

'Don't worry,' she said. 'You'll see what I mean at lunch.'

***

Nic held the gate open for Gia as she stepped through the rose-covered arch at the front of her family home. Fat pink roses spilled down in profusion on both sides of the latticed timber. A small east-facing courtyard was shaded from the early afternoon sun, and the overpowering fragrance of lavender drifted on the light breeze. Gia slowed her pace in front of him and Nic noticed her straighten her shoulders and take a deep breath. He was getting to know her little mannerisms very well. Although why she'd be so nervous with her own family, he found it hard to understand. He was envious of the close family relationship they seemed to have.

'Come on, let's get this over with.' She slipped her hand through his elbow and a smile appeared on her face. But it wasn't the impulsive smile he'd seen all week.

He was looking forward to seeing her with her family. He would support her and try to bolster her confidence and he was certainly going to talk up her talent. Whether it made a difference or not . . . time would tell.

The noise of a dozen or more people speaking at once met them as they walked through the stone-walled courtyard at the side of the old house. Gia slowed as they stepped onto the smooth green lawn and Nic put his hand on her back. She turned and gave him a sweet smile.

'Thank you,' she whispered, obviously feeling the support he was trying his best to give her. Nic frowned; it was such a shame if what Gia said about her family was true. Maybe she was oversensitive? Although he had heard her father dismiss her landscapes as unimportant. Why couldn't Gia's family see the person he saw? And support her? She was a confident, talented artist. It reminded him of the way his father looked down on him. He was a successful businessman, so why did his father dismiss every success he had and praise Antonio to the skies?

Okay, more than steered. More like directed. But he loved it now.

Nic understood. He loved his work at Carrara, overseeing the mining of the marble that was sold all over the world. Providing the marble for the creation of beautiful environments satisfied his creative needs. Being with Gia this week had been a wake-up call for him. Unexpectedly, watching Gia paint satisfied his creative urge, and despite his intentions, he didn't care if he painted or not. He also hadn't thought about the quarry or the contracts or his share prices.

Nic could admit to himself that yes, he could paint and, yes, he had talent, but he didn't have the passion that Gia did. Seeing the emotion that she invested in each stroke of her brush—it was almost Gia herself, and not her art, that spoke to him from her landscapes. Fulfilling his promise to his mother to come to Tuscany was beginning to put things into perspective for him. Maybe his father's decision had been the right path for Nic to follow. After all, he invested a similar passion into the business and his charity work.

Nic was lost in his thoughts when Gia turned and took his hand. They crossed the lawn toward two long tables set up beneath a green bower of verdant grapevines that shaded the tables from the sun. She led him to the end of the far table where there was a space. A tall woman with dark, curly hair just like Gia's looked at him with a wide smile on her face.

Gia reached over and kissed the woman's cheek '*Buongiorno,* Mamma. This is Nic. He is visiting our valley for a couple of weeks.' She turned back to him. 'Nic, this is my Mamma . . . Sylvia.'

The woman leaned forward and took Nic's hand and

kissed him on both cheeks. Nic smiled back at her.

'Una bella figlia di una madre bella.'

A beautiful daughter from a beautiful mother. Gia's eyes widened at his charm. 'Very smooth, Nic. Say the same to Nonna and you'll be loved for life.' She pointed to an elderly woman who was dozing in a rocking chair in the corner of the courtyard, oblivious to the hubbub of noise around her.

Nic smiled at her mother. 'It is a pleasure to be here. Thank you for letting me join your family lunch, Sylvia.'

'Pfft, Gia's friends are always welcome. But she never brings any home, do you, *bella*?' Sylvia waved a perfectly manicured hand. She was a very elegant woman and Nic watched with interest as she frowned at her daughter.

'Gia, where is your pretty dress? You know your father prefers to see you in a dress at lunch.'

'I'm sorry, Mamma. They are both in the wash.'

Her mother pursed her lips. 'If you would move back home to the village, you wouldn't have to worry. I could do your laundry for you.'

Gia simply smiled and didn't reply.

They settled at the table and introductions were made to a bevy of cousins, aunts, uncles, and finally to Gia's sister, Louisa, who arrived late with a man in tow.

Gia leaned across to Nic. 'That's good, that will take at

least half of the interest away from you.'

Nic leaned in and inhaled her strawberry fragrance. 'Your family is'—he had been going to say "wonderful" but Gia interrupted him.

'Overpowering, noisy, boisterous, and confident.'

Nic laughed and looked up just as Gia's father approached him.

'Gia! Welcome home.' He enfolded Gia in a bear hug and Nic smiled. It was as though Gia had been away for years and didn't work with her father each night. He looked around. Her brother didn't appear to be here yet.

Nic stood and held out his hand. 'Mauro. It is good to see you again.'

Gia's father shook his head and then beckoned him to follow him. 'Come. We have some fine wine over here.' When Gia stood to follow them, Mauro waved her away—rather rudely, Nic thought.

'Stay with the women, Gia. Your cousin has a new baby.' He beamed at the woman who was sitting across the table from Gia holding a small baby.

Nic frowned and before he could say he preferred to stay with Gia, she shrugged.

'Off you go, Nic. I am sure Papa wants to hear all about my show.' He was sure her smile was forced but she turned away to speak to her cousin. It was as though she was well used to being dismissed. No wonder she preferred to live alone. Nic followed Mauro over to the bar and watched as he deftly uncorked a bottle of red wine.

Mauro put the bottle on the tiled bar and reached for two glasses hanging from a shelf to the side. 'So, Gia tells me you work at Carrara?'

Nic nodded and tried to divert Mauro from the subject of his work. 'Yes, I live up there but I also try to spend some time in Florence where my brother lives.' He gestured to the crowd of people filling the garden. 'But my family is small and we rarely get together like this. I am very envious.'

Mauro beamed at him. 'Family and tradition. The most important things there are. We all get together at least once a month.'

Nic shook his head and accepted the glass of wine that Mauro handed him. 'About the only time our extended family sees each other is at funerals.' No matter how overbearing and smothering they might be, he *was* envious of Gia's family. The death of his mother had destroyed their family unit. Although he and Antonio saw each other often, it was primarily business driven. Nic wondered what it would be like to be a part of a family like this. A sense of loss filled him as he looked around at the children running around on the lush, green lawn, the older people nodding asleep in their chairs in the corner and the young mothers nursing their babies on their laps. The conversations were loud but happiness pervaded the whole terrace. The problem was it was all so tenuous. People died and the grief from their loss had more impact than family days like this.

Mauro raised his glass. 'Perhaps you may learn from your visit to our simple village and help your family try to get together more.'

Nic nodded. 'Perhaps.'

Looks like I've just gone up a notch in his estimation. Gaining Mauro's respect might make it easier to broach the subject of Gia's exhibition.

'So, you work for the Baldinis?' Mauro finished his wine and poured another glass. Nic sipped his slowly as Gia's father stared at him.

Now they were getting into dangerous territory. When Gia found out he was a Baldini, Nic wanted it to come from him, not from anyone else.

He nodded again. 'Yes, I work for the Baldinis.' Technically that was the truth, but discomfort settled in his chest. Not being completely truthful did not sit well with Nic. He believed in integrity in his business dealings, and never before in his personal life had he lied about anything.

'And you are interested in art, too?' Mauro's wide

forehead creased into a frown as if he couldn't understand.

'Yes, I have always been interested in art. Your daughter is very talented. Nic paused as unfamiliar nerves skittered through him as the inquisition continued. *Dio, don't tell me my cover is blown.* Nic put his wine down on the bar. 'I am very excited about helping Gia with an exhibition. She will do very well.'

Mauro waved his hand dismissively. '*Pfft.* If it makes her happy, I suppose I can agree to this little show.'

Nic bit back the angry words that rose in his throat. He hadn't come here to get her father's permission, but he didn't want to jeopardise Gia's relationship with him, either. He sipped at his wine again, nodded and changed the subject. Soon he was involved in a spirited discussion with Mauro about the shrinking Italian economy and the current recession.

Mauro thumped his glass onto the wooden bench beside them as he made a point.

'Yes, exactly,' Nic agreed. 'No one expected the poor growth and it does not bode well for the prime minister.'

'Nic?'

Nic hadn't noticed Gia's approach and he wondered how long she had been listening to their conversation. A frown creased her brow. As he watched she lifted one hand and smoothed down her wrinkled T-shirt. There was a smudge of something white near her right breast and he tried not to stare at it.

She noticed where he was looking and shrugged. 'It's baby vomit.'

Mauro grinned at Gia. 'So, you cuddled the *bambino*. Getting clucky, *cara*? Your Mamma already had Gabriel and Louisa when she was your age.'

Gia shot a wry glance at Nic. 'Yes, Papa, I cuddled the baby. I came over to tell you Mamma has put the food out. It is time to eat.'

They moved back to the table and Nic surveyed the spread of food in front of them. There was enough to feed at least twice the number that was here. The conversation washed around them, babies cried, and children squabbled at their feet. The noisier the gathering became, the more Gia seemed to withdraw into herself. Nic tried to engage her in conversation, but she just answered in monosyllables.

Eventually, he gave up and focused on his meal, wondering how much longer they would have to stay. He hated seeing Gia look so miserable.

Her father walked around filling up the glasses of the guests with the heady wine.

Nic put his hand over his glass. 'No more, thank you. I am driving.'

Mauro shrugged and moved to the cousin on the other side of Gia. 'And none for our little Gia. She cannot handle her wine.'

***

Papa's comment was the last straw for Gia. Nic had settled in all too well with her family and when she had gone over to tell them the food was served, his conversation with her father had surprised her. *The effect of the economy on business models? Where did that come from? Why the heck would Nic be trying to impress Papa?*

Gia's eyes narrowed. She had stood behind Nic listening to him talk to her father about the economy. Maybe she was being naïve but Nic's depth of knowledge of the economy was not what she would have expected from a quarry worker . . . or an artist.

A deep ache began in Gia's chest and she tried to pull herself out of this mood that her family always put her in. She simply didn't fit in and she never had. She tried her best to be what Papa wanted, but it just didn't work. And now here was her new friend and mentor—if you could call Nic that—agreeing with every word her father said, and apparently trying to impress him. Just someone else to tell fragile, little Gia what to do. Anger began a slow burn in her stomach, but it was directed at herself more than Nic. She had no one to blame for the way she was. If she wanted to be stronger and stand up for herself, she was the only one who could do it. For too long, she had been happy to fit in with what everyone else wanted.

As soon as the dessert was served, they would be able to leave without causing too much comment. The time dragged and despite Nic trying to get her to talk, Gia's mood sank lower. Finally, the children left the table to run on the grass again, the babies were carried inside for their afternoon nap and the women moved to clear the tables. Gia leaned over to Nic who was involved in an animated conversation with Louisa's new man.

'Are you ready to leave?'

The look of relief that crossed his face pleased her. Maybe Nic had been trying hard to fit in for her sake.

'Whenever you're ready.'

Gia stood and leaned over to say goodbye to Louisa. 'I'll see you next week.' Louisa only worked in the restaurant when there were many bookings.

Nic followed Gia to the other table where her parents were sitting.

Mauro stood and grasped Nic's hand. 'It was good to talk to you. Please come again.'

On their way to the car, Gabriel was hurrying down the path toward the house. They stopped, and he kissed Gia's cheek.

'You're late.' Gia looked at her brother and her mood

lifted. Gabriel's shirt was hanging from his jeans and there was a high flush on his cheeks. She bit back a grin. He looked like he'd been visiting his latest girlfriend. Good, it might take some of Papa's *bambino* pressure off her.

Gabriel reached out and shook Nic's hand. 'I believe that you would like me to set up the drinks at Gia's show.' He stared at Nic with a frown and Gia held back a sigh.

Why is everything to do with me a drama? What is wrong with my family? Or is it me?

Nic nodded and Gabriel glanced at her before turning his attention back to Nic. 'Perhaps you and I can meet one afternoon, Nic?'

That would be right. Don't include me. Gia huffed and walked over to Nic's car while they discussed a meeting time, their voices low. Finally, an agreement must have been reached, and they shook hands again before Nic followed her and started the car.

The road was busy with cars, bicycles, and pedestrians as the locals and tourists enjoyed the balmy afternoon. Gia felt a little better as they drove but she wanted to get her strange mood down on canvas.

Nic followed her into the cottage. He was quiet, too, and she wondered what had changed between them.

'So, I'm going to paint for a while. What about you?' Gia

turned and looked at him.

'I'll sit and watch if that's okay with you?' He'd been watching her paint every day for the past week and hadn't asked permission since that first day. Nic wandered over to the window and stared outside while she filled some of her bottles with water, and some with turpentine. He seemed distracted. Maybe her family had been too much for him but he'd seemed to enjoy himself while he was there.

Five minutes later Gia was in her own world.

Chapter Eighteen

Nic stretched out on the cushion-strewn sofa and watched Gia as she painted. There was something different about the way she painted this afternoon. She seemed distant. The bold strokes were gone and she was painting in soft pastels. Her brush was narrow-tipped and her strokes were gentle. A soft evening sky appeared on the canvas as he watched. Despite her slow strokes, the picture formed quickly. A haze surrounded the tops of the trees and the sky was soft with mist. Nic closed his eyes. Her talent blew him away.

He must have dozed off because a gentle hand on his shoulder woke him a while later. The room was almost dark and Gia had packed away her paints. She'd obviously showered; her hair was wet and her black curls were stuck in ringlets to her neck.

'Wake up, sleepyhead.' Her voice was soft as she leaned over him.

Nic reached up and pulled her down beside him on the sofa. 'You okay?'

'Yes, why?'

'You didn't seem to have a very good time this afternoon.'

He felt Gia's shoulders lift in a shrug as she lay beside him. 'Nothing different from usual. That's my family.'

Nic turned onto his side and looked at her. Gia's expression was still closed and his throat ached as a strange feeling wrapped around him. Reaching up, he tucked a strand of wet hair behind her ear. 'That was a very different painting you started before.'

She nodded and didn't speak but her eyes held his.

No matter what her mood was, Gia touched Nic in ways he'd never experienced before. He lifted her chin and placed a light kiss on her lips. Her mouth opened slowly beneath his and her tongue tentatively touched his lips. He pulled back and looked at her. Need tore through Nic, but it was a different need from the urgency of their passion of the past week. It was foolish to be nervous after all they'd shared but his hands trembled as he reached out to hold Gia against him. The strange feeling that embraced him filled his thoughts.

I want her. Not just for now, not just for the next few days, and not just for this exhibition. He wanted her to be a part of his life, and he wanted to share who he was with her. If he didn't, they had nothing. Any relationship would be based on falsity. It was bad enough that Gabriel had told him this afternoon he knew Nic was a Baldini. He had spent enough time in Florence and read the business magazines to recognise him. Despite the inquisition, Mauro didn't know. Nic had managed to extract a promise that Gabriel would not disclose that to either his father or to Gia; they were meeting tomorrow afternoon.

Not yet. He wanted her exhibition to go ahead. He wouldn't risk blowing that for her. But he was filled with uneasiness.

As Gia looked steadily back at him, he saw his feelings mirrored in her eyes. Did she know what he was thinking? She was so beautiful, so fresh and natural. It was her lack of artifice that had first attracted him and now that attraction was spiralling into a deeper need. Guilt for his lack of honesty with her settled in his gut like a stone, and he knew it was vital for whatever they had to be honest and share the truth about who he was. She was different from the other women who had tried to take advantage of his wealth. He was sure of it. But that was about all he was sure about as her eyes held his.

Can I trust her?

'Gia?' Digging deep for courage, he lifted her hand and pressed his lips to her paint-stained fingers. 'I need to talk to you.'

'What about?'

'Your commitment to your art and what a good person you are. What a *special* person you are. How I understand what your dreams are and how you want to follow them. How you *must* follow them and I need to talk to you about—'

Gia leaned into him and her voice was shaky as she interrupted him. 'Do you know what that means to me? To hear you say that? All my life, my family—my father, my mother, my brother, and my sister have treated me as though I don't have a thought of my own. They plan for me and they map my life out and they have no idea of who I am. I need to be myself and make my own decisions, my own mistakes.'

Nic closed his eyes. *And here am I about to map out her life for her.* 'Gia, I must tell you—'

'And now *you* want to tell me what to do. But not now.' She turned her lips into his palm and licked his skin. Fire whipped through Nic and he groaned. He lowered his mouth to hers and their kiss was soft but still full of desire. It soothed and eased the urgency of being honest with her, of telling her who he was. He would tell her later.

Time passed slowly and all Nic was aware of was Gia's soft body pressed against his. He ran his fingers through her wet tangled curls as she opened her mouth beneath his and welcomed him in as she tugged his shirt from his jeans.

Her hands moved slowly over his back as their lips stayed together. Gia murmured softly against his mouth as her fingers caressed his back beneath his shirt. Reluctantly he lifted his mouth from hers and sat up in one swift move, pulling his shirt over his head, unable to ignore the growing need for a minute more. Gia reached down and pulled her shirt up, lifting her head from the sofa as the shirt tangled in her wet hair. Nic reached down and pulled it over her head, grinning at the paint stains marring the new shirt she had worn to lunch. Then his mouth dried as her bare breasts filled his vision. *Coraggio,* the letters he had painted on her breasts—God, was it only a week ago— had faded and were almost gone. Now the only colour was in the dusky pink of her nipples.

A groan came from deep within Nic as her hands returned to his back and her fingers left a trail of fire on his skin. He was in no hurry; they had all night.

***

An hour later, Gia stretched and sighed and turned to face Nic. Her strange mood had lingered, reinforced by the gentle loving that Nic had shown her. The passion that usually took over when they had made love all this past week had still been there but Nic had been slow and gentle with her. Now, he lay quietly beside her as small ripples of pleasure ran through Gia, but he made no move to take his own pleasure yet. She lowered her hand and encircled him and his eyes widened.

'We'll have to go to the bedroom,' Nic said softly. 'My wallet is in there.'

Gia put on a mock pout, knowing full well what was in

his wallet before she smiled up at him and took his hand. 'Well, you'd better take me there.'

He pulled her up to her feet, but when his arms went around her, she lifted her face for another gentle kiss. She felt cherished . . . and valued. They stood there quietly with their arms around each other, each lost in their own thoughts. Gia eventually pulled away with a sigh. She was going to miss Nic when he went back to work. The sooner she could get to Florence, the better. She had to make this show the best she could. With Nic's help, she could do it.

***

Nic draped his arm casually around Gia's shoulder as they walked to her bedroom. She leaned into him and he buried his face in her hair as they stood by the side of the bed. Gia slid her hands down to her waist and slipped off her jeans.

Holy hell. Where had the little shy village girl disappeared to? She lay back on the bed and opened her arms to him. Nic groaned as he saw the expanse of bare skin in front of him.

'Do you ever wear underwear?' His voice was husky and he bent forward and put a hand on either side of her.

'Do you always wear jeans to bed?' Her smile was cheeky. As Nic undid the top button of his Levis, his phone rang in his back pocket.

'Ignore it.'

Nic grimaced and pulled his phone out and glanced down at the caller.

Shit. Antonio. Something was wrong. His brother wouldn't call otherwise.

'Hold that pose.' Nic flicked a saucy grin at Gia and stepped into the studio as he picked up the call. 'One second . . . maybe two,' he promised.

He put the phone to his ear but didn't get a chance to speak before Antonio's urgent words reached him.

'The deal's gone to shit.'

'Which one?' Nic lowered his voice.

'The only one. The one you went to New York for, Nic.'

'But that was in the bag.' Nic chose his words carefully, conscious of Gia in the next room. He glanced back into her bedroom; she had rolled over onto her stomach, her chin propped in her hand watching him. Two perfectly-shaped cheeks curved down to the tops of her thighs and Nic swallowed, trying to focus on his brother's next words.

'Not anymore.'

Shit, shit, shit. Nic knew he had to get out of here now and make some calls. He had signed the preliminary agreement with the Campbells, the largest bathroom and kitchen supplier in the States. Not only did the company's future export growth depend on the deal, Nic had invested a significant amount of his own fortune into it. If the deal fell through—and Nic still couldn't understand why it was at risk—the hospital funding would be in jeopardy, as well as the villa being used for the recuperation of children recovering from illness, as well as the artist retreat.

'Where are you? In Florence?' This time when he caught Gia's eye, Nic knew his smile was preoccupied.

'Yes, I got the call and came straight to the office. They've emailed the contract with the changes they want. I've printed it and I'm going through it now. Tad's on his way in.'

If Antonio had called their attorney in on the weekend Nic knew this was serious. He had no choice. He was going to have to leave. Antonio's next words dismissed any second thought he may have had. 'If we don't agree, the Faidiga family is lined up and ready to sign. The Campbells have already talked to them.'

'Bloody hell.' Nic hadn't been aware that the other big marble company in Carrara had been in negotiations with the Campbell Company in New York. Heads were going to roll over this monumental stuff up. Cold anger filled him. Someone had not kept him informed about every last detail of this deal.

'How long?' Gia was following every word of his conversation so Nic tried to keep his responses brief and ambiguous.

The timing of this absolutely sucks. If he'd been in

Florence or Carrara looking after things, he would have seen this coming.

'Eight hours.'

'I'm on my way. Wait for me.'

Nic disconnected the call and ran his hand through his hair. He was torn for the first time in his life; he wanted to stay with Gia but he had to leave. A woman had never had that power over him before and that fed his angst.

He had no choice. For the benefit of the company, the hospital, and the children, Nic had to go to Florence. He walked slowly into the bedroom and over to the bed. Gia's eyes didn't leave him. The organisation of the show was safely in Ben's hands so he didn't have to worry about the impact of his departure on the trustee vacancy.

'Is everything okay, Nic?' Her voice was soft and full of concern. 'You look so worried.'

Nic placed his hand on her bare hip and pushed away the desire that was still simmering in his blood. His mind was in Florence.

'I have to go.' He reached down for this shirt that lay on the floor.

'What's wrong?'

Shaking his head, he pulled his car keys out of his pocket. He leaned down to give her an absent kiss. 'I'll tell you about it later. Don't worry, it's nothing to do with you or the show. Just family stuff.'

***

Gia lay on the bed. When the sound of the Roadster faded down the hill, she slid from the bed and headed for the shower.

Her hair was half-dry and a tangled mess, so she soaked it with her strawberry-scented conditioner and then stood under the warm water, letting it saturate her. She tipped her head forward and the water soothed the tension at the back of her neck. It had been a difficult day and Nic leaving so suddenly with no explanation—not that she was really entitled to one—added to her confusion.

Nothing to do with you, he'd said. A little spurt of hurt rose in her gut. Just like the patronising way the men of her family treated her.

She wondered for the first time, if Nic was hiding something from her. Occasionally over the past few days, she'd been tempted to comment about how he had taken over this exhibition, but then she'd stop and think that if it wasn't for Nic, there would be no exhibition. Small things she hadn't taken much notice of in isolation all began to add up.

Am I making him into someone he's not? Have I put him in the role of rescuer because that is what I want?

The damsel in distress from their very first meeting?

Maybe she'd made her fairy tale dream come true? Her world was always coloured in the tones and hues of what she believed, and Gia knew she was too trusting. When Papa had refused to fund her move to Florence, his words had cut deep, even though he had been trying to be kind.

You are living in a fantasy world, bella. *It would never work out.*

Was Nic's promise the right answer? Or should she just keep slogging away and saving her money? Was she only dreaming and looking for the easy way? And would Nic really follow through with what he'd said? Maybe he was a dreamer, just like she was? Was she letting him take too much control?

Gia closed her eyes and tipped her head back as confusion overwhelmed her. The warm water ran in soft trails down her cheeks. Why had Nic left so suddenly with little explanation? Was this all destined to end up in tears?

Nic and his support of her show was a way to escape this life she was stuck in. Was she reading too much into what had happened between them? A heavy feeling of pending disappointment settled in her chest and Gia put her hand to her breast and glanced down.

Only a pale pink outline of the letters remained. The scarlet paint had worn off through the week. Gia reached for the bar of soap on the self behind her and slowly scrubbed the last traces of the word away. It was time to stand on her own two feet. Nic had presented her with this marvellous opportunity. He was going to help her and he'd promised to call the man who would then help her plan her future if she sold her paintings at the exhibition.

Until Nic gave her reason not to, she would trust him.

Gia scrubbed away the last tiny speck of paint on her breast and shook her head.

Coraggio.

Not *if* she sold her paintings. *When* she did.

***

Nic and Antonio had salvaged the deal and their copy of the contracts had been signed, witnessed, and sent back to New York with a couple of hours to spare before he hit the freeway and headed back to Castellina. The ball was in the Campbell's court now, but Nic was confident they had solved the problem. But he couldn't allow himself to get cocky until the deal was final. He could have handled it by phone, but in his usual way, he needed to be there and have total control. Now, with that sorted out, he could focus on Gia's show and then get back to work at the end of the week.

Almost losing that contract had been a huge wake-up call for him. He'd had a lot of time to think on the drive back down to Castellina. The traffic had been quiet and a light shower of rain had wet the road and kept him alert. His mind had been spinning as he'd admitted to himself what it would have meant to lose that deal. He had to prioritise his life. Telling his brother to leave him alone while he was off painting had been selfish and naive. They had a billion-dollar company to run together. Playing around with his art was well and good, but he couldn't put a deal like that at risk because he was chasing a gypsy's story.

Mamma, I love you. But you were wrong. Now I can see where I need to be.

It's time for honesty. I need to be upfront with Gia.

Nic arrived back at Gia's cottage just before midnight and parked the car on the grass. A low light shone through the studio window and he smiled. It looked like she was still working. Anticipation ran through him as he stood on the front porch and tapped on the door.

'Come.' Gia's soft voice was distracted. Nic pushed the door open; Gia stood in front of her easel, the tip of her tongue resting on her bottom lip as she stared at the landscape in front of her.

Nic walked over, slid his arms around her waist and buried his face in her curls. The strawberry scent was so overpowering his mouth watered. Gia turned in his arms and Nic lifted his hand to wipe away a single smudge of paint on her cheek.

'Hello, *bella.*' He dropped a light kiss on her lips and smiled down at her as her stomach grumbled. 'Have you eaten?'

She shook her head. It was no wonder she was so slim. When she was engrossed in her work, Nic noticed that she forgot to eat.

'I guessed that would be so. I brought you a baguette.' Nic had his story ready to explain his rush trip to Florence, but Gia didn't ask him anything.

She crossed to the fridge and poured them both a wine before sitting on the sofa with her feet tucked beneath her. A small smile crossed her face as she tucked her hair back behind her ear, and slid those ugly glasses up her nose. She unwrapped the baguette and inhaled the smell of the fresh bread with a sigh.

'My favourite, thank you.'

'I'm pleased. I chose well.' A warm and fuzzy feeling settled somewhere between Nic's chest and his stomach. It was as though he'd come home. He tried to push the feeling away.

'While I was waiting for you, I chose the paintings for my show.' Gia spoke with her mouth full and Nic grinned at her.

'Fantastic! Two weeks from today. It will be a spectacular success. Everyone will be so proud of you as you are introduced to the art world.' That was all he wanted for Gia, to launch her successful career.

It was. Nothing more.

The happiness on Gia's face hit Nic like a punch in the gut. On the trip home, he'd given a lot of thought to where he and Gia had been heading. The problem with the contract had pulled him back to reality. He wasn't going to risk a relationship with her. Business was his life. It was something he had control over. It would be hard to leave her after the show but he couldn't risk it. He could control the business—he couldn't control life or death. When his mother died, he had vowed he would never put himself in a position where he would end up like his father. Gia's newfound assurance would probably take a dive if he revealed the truth now. But it had to be done.

Before I leave for good.

Maybe.

But more than that can I risk the chance of losing her?

What do I want?

He knew that Gia's newfound assurance would disappear if he revealed the truth now. Her mood had been strange when they'd left her parents' house. He was going to keep things as they were, but not telling her did not sit comfortably with him either, and he had convinced himself that it was for her own sake as much as his. Her confidence had built so much over the past few days. Nic wasn't prepared to see it crumble.

He looked up as Gia scrunched up the paper from the baguette and brushed the crumbs from her lap. 'And I've thought of all the other things we need to do. Tomorrow, I am putting my easel and paints away and I'm going to start getting this place cleaned up.'

She didn't notice his preoccupation and Nic pulled his attention back to her. 'Do I get the impression that cleaning up the studio is a rare event and that being organised is not something you would usually do?'

'You'd be right. It drives my family crazy. I'm always late, and when I get immersed in a painting I forget to go places.' She tipped her head to the side. 'Look at the chaos I live in. What about you, Nic? I get the impression that your life is nicely organised. Look at you, you always look perfect.'

Dangerous topic here.

He reached out, picked up Gia's hand, and brought it up to his mouth Her eyes were alight and vitality filled her expression. At lunch, she had been a shadow of this woman. Her family had told her she couldn't drink because of how silly it made her. All her father could talk of was a husband and babies and dismissed her talent as unimportant. *I suppose I can agree to this little show*, he'd said.

Nic looked at Gia. There was no way he was going to burst her bubble. Okay, he was chickening out, but it was for her own good.

'Oh, yes, I'm organised. My mother—God rest her soul—

was very much into astrology. According to my star sign, I'm organised and always have to be in control.' Nic shook his head with a laugh. 'But I don't believe in all that star sign crap. I mean how can you generalise and say one-twelfth of the population all share the same traits?' He stared across the top of Gia's head, looking at the landscapes now stacked neatly against the wall. 'She always said I was a true Cancerian . . .'

'And what does that say about you?' Her voice was soft.

'Passionate, volatile, exciting.' Nic leaned over and pulled Gia across to him so that her back was against his chest. He lowered his lips and murmured against her ear. 'But I do believe in some of it . . . they say a Cancerian male needs pampering every minute of the day.'

Gia twisted around in his arms and laughed. 'Oh, do *they*? I've always wondered who those mysterious experts are. Poor Mamma is always worried about what *they* will say or what *they* will think, especially if I left the village.'

'Oh, trust me. *They* are right in this case because if I'm pampered, I respond by being chivalrous.'

'Well, you are certainly that.' Gia crawled up so that she was now sitting on his lap, and Nic had a less-than-chivalrous reaction.

Gia wriggled against him 'Oh, my. You do look tired. How about I look after you for a change?' Her voice was soft and her sultry eyes were fixed on his.

Nic closed his eyes and let Gia pamper him.

Chapter Nineteen

Helping Gia clean up her studio filled the last days before the exhibition. They carted garbage, moved canvases, and when Gia decided that the studio walls needed to be painted white as a backdrop for her landscapes, they drove into Siena to buy the paint. They laughed, they painted together, they made love in the afternoon, at night, and in the mornings. Nic began to realise that leaving Gia was not going to be so easy but he pushed aside the thought until the very last afternoon.

On the Sunday afternoon before her show, he left her painting the walls and drove up to the villa to collect a few things he'd not brought down to her cottage. He was supposed to go back to the office in Carrara tomorrow to deal with yet another issue that had arisen. A strange feeling lodged in Nic's throat and he frowned. The thought of leaving Gia was hard. He'd spent almost every day and night with her. His planned summer break had come to an early end.

Nic shook his head as he pushed open the door of the villa. What had happened here had not been in his plan for his summer in Tuscany. The food he'd ordered was still sitting untouched in the pantry and refrigerator. As much as it was going to be hard to leave Gia and go back to work, he was looking forward to her show next weekend. He knew she would move to Florence. It was her dream and she would sell enough of her work to fund that. Maybe they could stay in touch when she moved there. No strings attached. After the show, he would tell her who he was.

***

'I'll be back next weekend.' Nic pressed gentle kisses onto her neck and Gia closed her eyes. 'Only seven more days until your show.'

Finally, he pulled away and climbed into the car.

She held his hand through the window of his car as he held the steering wheel with the other. 'I'll miss you, but I have plenty to do if I'm going to be ready by next weekend.' She fought to keep her voice steady. How could she have become so attached to this man in only a few weeks?

'I'll call tonight.'

She leaned in and kissed him one more time before he put the car into gear and backed out through the gate. As Nic's Roadster disappeared around the last bend in the road Gia brushed away the tears that spilled over her cheeks. She listened until the motor faded to silence and the night was quiet. Nic had planned to leave before dark, but one thing led to another and they had ended up in Gia's bed. He was as reluctant to leave as she was to see him go, and he'd held her close as they lay together.

She rubbed her arms as she slowly walked back inside. Goose bumps rose on her skin as doubt flooded through her. He said she could trust him and he had given her no reason not to, but a persistent feeling that something was not right wouldn't leave her. She shook it off; it was just that his holiday had come to an early end for some reason and she had to adjust to him leaving.

She knew the week would fly by. She was going to be busy, and Nic had promised to call each night. There was one more painting she wanted to complete, and she had to work at the restaurant every night, though she had begged Papa to give her Saturday night off and, surprisingly, he had agreed.

She pushed open the door into her empty cottage and headed straight for her easel.

***

The week did fly by and Gia became more nervous as each day passed, though she hadn't let on how she was feeling when Nic had called. On Friday morning a crew of workmen knocked at her door and waited for her to tell them where to hang her paintings. As soon as they were finished, she'd called Nic.

'You didn't have to do that. I had asked Gabriel and Papa to come and help me.'

'No, it has to be perfect.'

'But, Nic, it doesn't really have to be. It must be so expensive. I will pay you back everything.' Guilt ran through her. She was worried about the amount of money he must have spent setting everything up. He had taken control but she had let him.

Nic laughed and a tremble ran down Gia's legs. Even his voice from hundreds of kilometres away sent shivers down to her belly.

'We'll see. We need to get this show in place and then see where your dreams take you.'

Gia sighed. She knew where she wanted to be.

Wherever Nic was.

'The caterers will be there early on Sunday. And Gia… I'm sorry. Something has come up.' Her stomach plummeted and she waited. 'I can't make it tomorrow.'

'But you will be here Sunday?'

'Of course. I wouldn't miss it for the world. I'll be there early. Don't worry, everything is organised. I'm bringing my friend with me, too. The one who will help with the sales. What are you going to wear?'

Gia grinned. 'Oh, I just thought one of my black skirts and a white shirt would do.'

Nic's voice was low and husky. '*Hmm.* Well, maybe I'll have to take them off you and dress you when I get there. I'll be early.'

She retreated to her easel and banished the disappointment by painting a new landscape.

Saturday passed slowly. Gia sighed; she would only have a short time with Nic on Sunday when everyone else was there. Who everyone else was, she didn't have a clue. Her parents had cancelled the usual family lunch, and Mamma had invited most of the village. Papa had taken to bragging about it to the patrons of the restaurant each night.

Nic didn't call and didn't answer when she called him, and the doubt set harder in her chest as she climbed into her lonely bed late on the night before the exhibition.

Why did I ever agree to this?

And then she tossed and turned all night wondering where he was and why he hadn't come, and why he didn't call. She closed her eyes and summoned her courage against all the doubts flooding her mind.

She was woken by a knock at the door just after seven on Sunday, and she pulled on her robe and hurried out. The events team that Nic had sent had arrived— and they were unloading a huge van.

Oh my God. Gia put her hand to her mouth. This was really happening. She let out a sigh of relief as a cloudless sky met her gaze. It was a beautiful Tuscan summer's day. The sky was a pale blue and a gentle breeze puffed the lavender fragrance across from the nearby fields. Her flowers had bloomed in the past week and the lawn was green and lush. A second truck arrived and parked behind the first one, and three men unloaded two portable toilets. She held back a giggle; this was so not Castellina. Shaking her head, she went back inside, at a loss, feeling as though events had spiralled out of her control. She wandered around her studio. Looking at her work mounted on the newly painted walls was surreal.

An hour later Gia came back out and looked around in amazement. Nic had obviously given the workers explicit instructions on how the garden was to be set up. It was a little more formal than what she would have chosen to do herself, but she should be grateful to him for all he'd done for her. The garden and studio had been transformed into a stylish and formal exhibition space. The tables were now draped with white linen cloths and urns filled with fresh flowers were now positioned around the garden. A long table with glistening crystal champagne flutes was along the shaded wall. Her legs trembled and she put her hands over her face.

Can I do this? Can I really do it? Showing her work to her family and a few patrons in a village restaurant was very different from having a real show.

She could not believe the organisation Nic had managed

from afar. He'd not even told her what to expect, except that a few people would be turning up to help. He had taken total control. Her phone rang and she hurried inside.

'How are you feeling, *bella*?' Nic's voice grounded her.

'I'm good. And oh, Nic, I am so nervous, too.'

'We've just turned off the main road. We'll be there in half an hour.'

Happiness hit her in a huge burst, and she hugged herself as she headed for the shower.

After her shower, Gia dressed. She had found a scarlet silk dress in one of the small dress stores in the village and it fit perfectly. Shoes had been a problem, and she'd called on her sister, Louisa, to borrow a pair. Louisa had taken one look at the dress and taken her straight to her leather shop in the village.

But now, as she took a final look at herself in the mirror, an unfamiliar sight met her eyes. A confident woman dressed elegantly stared back at her. Gia smiled at her unexpected poise. No sign of nerves showed on her face, even though her stomach was in knots. She took a deep breath and stepped out through the door as a large black SUV pulled to a stop outside the gate. An unfamiliar man stepped from the driver's side, and Gia's heart rate almost doubled as the other door opened and Nic stepped out. Her mouth dried as he walked across to her. Just like the first time she'd seen him, sunshades covered his eyes, but his lips were turned into a huge smile. A formal dark suit, a pale-blue shirt, and a silver tie had turned him into a creature of sartorial elegance. She hitched a breath. This man was way too elegant for her. This wasn't her Nic; he was a stranger and she suppressed a nervous shiver.

'Stop it.' Nic leaned forward and his breath brushed her ear. 'I can read your thoughts.' His lips slid across her cheek in a soft kiss before he straightened. 'Gia, this is Ben. He's here to help with the sales.'

The tall man beside Nic took her hand and shook it. 'A pleasure to meet you.'

Gia nodded nervously. *To help with the sales.* 'I hope there are some.'

Nic put his arm around her shoulder. 'Come, we'll get Ben set up and then you can show me around.'

After he'd set up his laptop and some sort of wireless device beside it, Ben left them to go and look at her paintings.

Nic led Gia outside to the garden and held her hands. 'You look absolutely stunning.'

She raised a shaking hand to her hair and smoothed back a stray curl that never stayed in place. 'I am so nervous. What if nobody comes? What if they hate my work? What if nothing sells?'

Nic put his fingers on her lips. '*Ssh.* I know people are

coming down from Florence. And I know you are going to be a sensation.'

Gia lifted her hand and cupped Nic's cheek. 'Oh, Nic. I so hope I don't let you down. You have gone to so much trouble and spent so much money. I *will* repay you from these sales, even though we never found time to have a written agreement. You must take my word for it.'

A strange look crossed his face, but his words reassured her. 'I told you I was going to support you. And I have no doubt that you are going to be an incredible success. Just wait and see.'

***

Nic stood back a few hours later and watched his shy little waitress turn into a butterfly. Everything was sold and Ben had the twelve landscapes Nic had bought on the side. He stood in the shade and listened to the enthusiasm of the guests as they gushed to Gia about her work.

'Fresh.'

'Exciting.'

'Emotive.'

Mauro crossed the lawn to stand beside Nic. The rest of Gia's family had come and gone. Nic had watched the doubt in their expressions turn to surprise as they witnessed the reaction of the crowd and the sold stickers go up on each painting.

'My little Gia is a surprise. She has turned into a

butterfly.'

Nic lifted his glass to Mauro. 'That is just what I was thinking. A beautiful butterfly.'

Her father's eyes narrowed. 'So, Nic, what are your intentions with my daughter? You live a long way away. I would hate to see you break her heart.'

'We are friends and I support her work.' Nic held the other man's eyes steadily.

Mauro nodded and looked thoughtfully across the garden where his daughter posed for a photograph with one of the private photographers that Nic had hired. 'My daughter has gained a lot of poise. I thank you for that. I think.' Mauro shook his hand and turned to the gate. 'She is busy and I must go to work. Would you like to come down for dinner later?'

Nic nodded. 'Yes, that would be good.'

Mauro smiled and waved as he ambled across the garden. The crowd was thinning and the waiters began to pick up the empty glasses that were scattered around the tables in the garden. Nic waited until Gia finished with the photographer and looked across at him with a brilliant smile. Her eyes were sparkling and her cheeks were flushed. As she walked across to him, she smiled and nodded confidently at the people who congratulated her.

'Oh, Nic.' Gia stood beside him and clasped her hands in

front of her chest. 'There is not one painting left.' Her eyes were wide and her lips softly parted. 'I hate saying goodbye to them, but knowing that people want them is incredible. Every one of my landscapes has been sold and I cannot believe the prices that Ben put on them.' She spun around in excitement and the scarlet silk twirled high around her long legs. 'People bought *my* work. Me! Gia Carelli! And they want more.'

Nic reached out and pushed her curls behind her ear. 'Of course, they do. I told you that would happen.'

'I am so happy. How will I ever repay you for what you've done for me?'

'I have something I want to tell you when everyone is gone. Your father has asked us for dinner, but I would like some time alone with you first.'

Gia's eyes were shining. 'And I have a special surprise for you, too.'

Nic turned her around and pushed her gently toward the crowd. 'But first, go and talk to your admirers. See that lady over there with the silver dress? Jolie is the art writer for the *La Nazione* and she is waiting for an interview.'

Gia gasped and put her hands to her mouth. 'But that is the biggest newspaper in Florence.'

'That's right. So don't keep her waiting.' Nic put his hands out to steady Gia as she grabbed his face and kissed him on the lips.

'Oh, you are so good to me.' She spun around with a happy laugh and Nic watched as she hurried across to the journalist and became engrossed in a deep conversation.

'You've found another little protégée, I see, Nic.' He turned to find Ben beside him.

'I have. Ben, don't tell her how many I bought, okay? I want it to be a surprise.' Nic had already selected walls, in his apartment in Florence, for each of the landscapes.

'Not a problem. I'll just go and pack them up and put them in the car so she doesn't see.'

'Appreciate it.' As Nic turned to look for Gia his phone vibrated in his pocket, and he pulled it out with a frown.

Antonio? What now?

'Yes?' Nic put the phone to his ear as he walked across to stand by Ben's SUV.

'Nic, where are you?'

'I'm in Tuscany at an art show. What's so urgent?'

'The deal has gone to shit.'

'What? What deal?'

'The New York deal.'

'Again? What the hell has happened now? I thought they were signing tomorrow?'

'They were. Tad's about to leave for the airport.

Apparently, there was something in a gossip magazine about you dumping old man Campbell's daughter and he didn't like it.'

'What the hell? I took her out for dinner once.' Nic had enjoyed her company but it had been a business dinner, not a date. 'I barely know the woman.'

'Well, Campbell didn't like it and he's about to pull out. You'd better make some very quick calls.'

Nic clenched his fist and hit it on the top of Ben's car. He could not handle it when things didn't go to plan.

'Are you there, Nic? Are you coming to the office? Tad's here waiting for your instructions.' Antonio's voice annoyed him.

'Shit, yes. I'm on my way. But Antonio? I need a favour. Can you go up to Carrara tomorrow and look after the place? Normally, I wouldn't worry but there was some strike action brewing on Friday.' He wouldn't tell Gia he was coming back in case anything else came up.

'Are you going to New York with Tad?'

Nic closed his eyes. 'Probably not. I'll try and figure it out from the office but I need to come back down here tomorrow.'

'Why back there?'

'I just do.'

'Okay. Hurry up. Tad will have to catch the later flight.'

'I'm on my way.' Ice-cold fingers closed around his throat at the thought of losing the deal.

But even more so, the thought of leaving Gia on this night when they should be celebrating her success broke his heart. That was even worse than the thought of the Campbell deal falling through.

Chapter Twenty

Gia's excitement about the success of the show had tempered her disappointment at Nic's sudden departure for a while. He'd come over to her while she'd been talking to the journalist and pulled her aside. His mysterious brother "needed" him again, and he'd kissed her and left before she'd had time to ask any questions. Ben had gone with him so she didn't even know yet how successful the day had been.

The caterers had packed up, the last person had left, and Gia was alone. She wandered into the bedroom and pulled the scarlet silk dress over her head. She pursed her lips and shrugged as it hit the floor. There'd been no need for the lacy scarlet underwear she'd put on for Nic. He hadn't even seen it.

Gia's mood vacillated. Nic was a good man and look what he had done for her. But he'd just left . . . again . . . without an explanation. Her high from the show flattened out. Her family had left, and they expected her to go to the restaurant for dinner. All she wanted was to celebrate the success of the day with Nic. Yet, here she was all alone… And again, he'd left her. It was almost as though he had something to hide.

She pulled off the lacy underwear and pulled on a pair of loose cotton pants and a T-shirt and wandered out to the studio.

The bare walls left her hollow. It was as though her life had left with the paintings—or was it Nic's absence that had left the huge emptiness in her chest? Gia straightened her shoulders and wandered back into the bedroom. She stared at Nic's painting.

No. I am not going to lose my confidence ever again. I am not going to sink back into that shy person.

Her first encounter with Nic had been a sign of things to come; he had rescued her. Going back to the studio, she pushed open the door and went to the small shed. She carried her easel and one small table back into the studio before pulling her paints out. The painting she had hidden from Nic, the one that she had begun after he had made such gentle love to her that night, was for him. Even if nothing more came from meeting Nic, she wanted him to have a memory of what they had shared when he had set her on her path to her dream. Just as she would never let the painting that he had done go, no matter what happened.

Gia painted all night, and as the sun sent its first slivers of rosy light onto her bare white walls she stepped back and stretched her shoulders. A feeling of satisfaction ran through her. She had no doubt this was the best thing she had ever painted. It was also the first landscape she had ever put herself in. Even she could see the emotion between them and she knew it was real. She would hug that to herself until Nic returned. She had no doubt that he would. Her faith in him was the catalyst that had let Gia's faith in her art blossom. The future was beckoning, and she was filled with anticipation. She sang aloud as she cleaned up her paints and set the painting against the wall before she headed for the shower. Her hands and arms were covered with paint and probably her face, too. As she stood beneath the water, she kept one eye on the phone, which she put on the floor on her towel, but it remained silent.

As she dried off, her heart jumped as the sound of a car coming up the road drifted through the open window.

Nic's back.

Dressing quickly, she hurried to the door and opened it, and tried not to look too disappointed as Papa stepped from his car, clutching a newspaper to his chest, followed closely by Gabriel.

'Papa?' Excitement filled her as she saw it was *La Nazione.* 'Is my show in the paper already?' As she grabbed it from him, she looked up and saw the frown on his face and more disappointment flooded through her. A successful show, all of her paintings sold, and still her father had no joy for her. She turned away and opened the paper, searching for the lifestyle section where the exhibitions were reported.

'Gia.' Her father touched her arm. His brow was wrinkled in a frown, and he ran a weary hand across his face. '*Bella,* listen to me.' His voice was sad.

'What is it?' She slowly put the paper down and looked at her father.

'This will show you that you must listen to your family,' he said. 'We know best. Always.'

Cold prickled through Gia's blood, and her breath hitched as her father picked the paper up and held it in front of her.

'What? What is this?' A picture of Nic kissing her goodbye yesterday filled the centre of the front page. 'What are you showing me?'

'Gia, calm down.' Gabriel walked over and held her arms. 'I am sorry I let you down. I knew who he was all along and he made me promise—'

'Who? What are you talking about Gabriel?' She snatched the paper from his hands and scanned the headline in disbelief.

Has Millionaire CEO Nic Baldini Lost His Touch?

'*Baldini?*' Her voice dropped to a whisper, and she ignored her father when he tried to speak. '*Nic Baldini!*'

Striding over to the table, Gia spread the paper flat and put her hands on either side, bracing herself. A cold shiver ran through her, and her knees trembled as she read the headline article. She swallowed as her stomach threatened to rise into her throat.

'*Has the Italian Angel lost his touch? The latest deal of*

the Baldini brothers is on shaky ground. What was to be the biggest marble contract for the business duo is now in doubt. Rumour has it that his girlfriend, Jennifer Campbell, the daughter of Managing Director of the New York Campbell Company is less than happy with Nic's continued absences to his Tuscan love nest with his latest protégée, unknown artist Gia Corelli. But does it matter? The Angel has been appointed to the vacancy on the board at the Uffizi Gallery, so maybe his attention will be elsewhere from now on. Watch this space.'

Gia screwed the paper up and threw it on the floor in disgust. 'Corelli! They can't even spell my name right.'

She paced the room as her father watched cautiously.

'*Latest* protégée? How many were there before me!' Rage and grief fought for precedence. Taking a deep breath, Gia tried to compose herself. She had kidded herself thinking she was special to Nic. It was the most emotion she had ever shown in front of her father. 'Well, Papa. You were right. I was wrong all along.'

Her father held his hand out to her, but Gia shook her head. 'I have to go and see him. Will you please lend me your car? I will not be treated like this.'

'I will come with you. Where is he?'

'No. I will go alone. I am not the shrinking violet you think I am. And don't worry. It is well known that the Baldini brothers live in an old Medici palace near the city. I will find him.' Gia gritted her teeth. 'If it takes all day, I will find him.'

'I will come with you.' Gabriel's voice was quiet, and Gia nodded as he took the car keys from his father.

'I will walk back to the village. You drive carefully.' Papa stood at the door and looked at her. 'You will both be back in time to work at the restaurant tonight?'

Gia's world crumbled as her father put her future into words. She nodded slowly. 'Yes, Papa. I will be back in time.'

***

Nic woke late and headed to the kitchen for a coffee. The muted sounds of the Monday morning traffic from the *Via dei Serragli* had finally woken him from a deep sleep. As he passed through the foyer on the way to the kitchen, he grinned. Gia's paintings were lined up along the walls inside the door. As soon as he'd showered, he was going to drive down to see her and make up for leaving her yesterday. It was time to be truthful; the exhibition had been a huge success and it was all due to Gia's talent, not his organisation or the Baldini name.

He and Antonio had spent hours on the phone last night, dealing and negotiating. Finally, they had convinced Campbell that the gossip magazines were not to be believed and that they were trustworthy. It was not until Campbell had called his daughter—who was on holiday in London—that he'd agreed to seal the deal.

After Nic drank his coffee, gazing out over the small courtyard garden between his and Antonio's apartments, he headed for his bathroom. The sooner he got on the road, the better. Being a Monday, the trip to Tuscany would be slow. As he crossed the foyer, Ben called him into the study.

'What are the chances of this making it to Tuscany this morning?' He held the newspaper up. Nic hadn't heard Ben arrive. He must have started work early this morning. He groaned when he saw the photo and the headline.

'*Fanculo*. How did they get hold of that?' The last thing he wanted was the paparazzi hounding him again. And it was such bad timing.

Ben shrugged. 'The photographer must have thought he could make some quick money. I'm sorry, Nic.'

'*Dio*.' Nic rubbed his hands over his face. 'I only got the call from the director last night. In the middle of all of the contact negotiations.'

Ben shrugged. 'They pay well for scoops. Someone let the cat out of the bag.'

Nic waved his hand. 'It's okay. Gia won't see it. I'm going down there this morning. Now that she's had the show and the deal is settled, I'll come clean and tell her everything.'

'I hope it all works out for you. I've never seen you so

happy. She's more than a protégée to you, isn't she?'

Nic stared at his PA. 'No, we're just friends and I helped her out.'

Ben shook his head and grinned. 'I think you're kidding yourself there, boss. The sparks between the two of you almost set the place on fire yesterday. You looked so proud of her success.'

Nic stood beneath the shower, trying to wake up enough to drive out of the city. It had been a long and late night. He closed his eyes as he reached for the shampoo, imagining what it would be like to have Gia living in Florence. He whistled as contentment settled in his chest. So long as she was cool with him being a Baldini. He was sure of her now, surer than anything he had been of in his life. He'd hated lying to her, and he hoped that she would understand why he had not told her who he was before this. Now that she was a success, he would convince her that it was her talent alone that had got her to that point. He'd simply provided a framework for her to show her brilliant work to the world. Nic frowned as a doubt niggled at him. The way her family treated Gia had left her self-assurance so raw. It was past time for him to realise that he had to let go of that fear of putting his heart in someone else's hands. He caught sight of himself in the large mirror as he quickly towelled off. A goofy grin spread across his face.

I love her.

Nic bypassed his usual grooming and pulled on a pair of jeans and a T-shirt before he grabbed his keys and headed back downstairs. Ben was talking to someone in the foyer, and Nic backtracked, heading for the back door to the garage.

'His PA?' Nic stopped dead as Gia's voice came up the stairs. It *couldn't* be Gia, but it sounded like her. How the hell did she know where to find him? Nic walked slowly down the stairs as Ben's calm voice mixed with Gia's. It *was* her. Nic stared at her and cold dread pooled in his gut.

Gia was clutching a newspaper in her hands and she looked at him. Her eyes were wide and clear, but her cheeks were flushed.

'Hello, *Signore* Baldini. How lovely to visit you in your own home.' Her tone was scathing and Nic crossed the marble tiles and put his hand out to her but she pushed it away. 'It was very kind of Ben, your *PA,* to let me in.'

Ben shot Nic an apologetic look as he backed out of the foyer into the study and closed the door. As the door closed, one of Gia's paintings slid from the wall and tipped over, lying face up in the middle of the tiles. She looked along the wall at the row of her landscapes. Her sharp indrawn breath was followed by one word. *'Bastardo.'*

Nic grabbed her arms and looked down at her beautiful face as her tears began to fall. 'Listen to me, Gia.' He nodded to the paper. 'I can explain that. I can explain everything. There is no woman.'

She shook her head and her curls covered her face. 'No.'

Nic ran his hand through his hair in frustration and sought the right words but her cold voice stopped him.

Gia pushed her hair back with both hands as she turned to him. 'I could have accepted this'— she threw the paper at him and it slid down the front of Nic's legs and landed on the floor— 'the lying about who you are for whatever reason, maybe you just wanted to be someone else for a while. *Dio*, I've wanted to do that every day of my life. But'—she gestured to her paintings— 'I'll never forgive you for this. No one bought my paintings. *You* took them. You betrayed my trust.'

'Listen to me. I didn't. Not all of them.' Nic grabbed her arms, but Gia shoved him away and stepped back. Gabriel stepped forward but she shook her head.

She held up her hand. 'No. Just no. You know how much my family protects me for "my own good".'

Nic cursed himself to hell and back as her voice broke.

'I thought you knew me. The *real* me. I was beginning to think you might even love me. But you just felt sorry for me and wanted to protect me like everyone else. Didn't you?' Gia crossed to the wall and put her foot through the middle of one of the canvases. 'This? All this is just a waste of time. They were right.'

'No, you're wrong. Gia, you have—'

'Stop it, Nic. You're worse than they are.' She scrubbed at her eyes and covered her face and Nic's heart shattered when she removed her hands and looked at him, hatred filling her dark eyes.

'At least my family does it out of misguided love. You, you just can't help being the *Italian Angel.* You have to be saving someone. Don't you? I read it all. Was I just another one of your projects?' Gia turned around, looking for the door. 'No, don't answer that. I don't care. I'll never know if my first showing was a success of my own doing and if people really like my art or they were there to win your favour, right?'

Nic stared at her, unable to lie any more.

'Oh, my God! You set the whole thing up, didn't you? It was all fake, wasn't it? You invited all of those people?'

Nic had no choice. The time for lies was over. If there was any chance of salvaging what he had with Gia, he had to tell the truth.

He nodded mutely and saw the light in her eyes die. 'Yes, I did invite a special group but I had my reasons—'

'*Pah,* so it was rent-a-crowd! Did anyone else even *buy*

my work?' She stomped her foot. 'How dare you, Nic.' Her voice dropped to an anguished whisper. 'How dare you play with my life!' Her shoulders slumped in front of him. 'No more. Don't you ever, ever come near me again. You have crushed me, Nic. I thought you had found the real me, but it doesn't exist, does it? I have no art. I have no talent.'

Gabriel put his arm around her, led her out and the door closed behind them. Nic stared at the canvases around him. Her passion was on every one, for the world to see. He pulled the door open and ran to the old car that was parked illegally on the side of the narrow street.

'Gia! Wait. I have to explain to you. Please!' he begged. 'You have it all wrong.'

She sat rigid in the passenger seat, staring straight ahead. She spoke without turning to him.

'Just leave me alone. I cannot bear it.'

He shook his head. 'No! You must listen to me. Let me explain.'

Her lips were white and Nic's heart ached at the pain in her voice. Finally, she turned to look at him. 'I will never ever forget what you have done for me, but I will be forever grateful. I am no artist. You helped me realise that. Gabriel, take me away from here.' Her eyes were sad as she stared at Nic. 'Take me home where I belong.'

Chapter Twenty-One

Nic drove slowly up the hill to the villa. He was going to stay here while he persuaded Gia that he loved her, no matter how long it took. Deals didn't matter. Gia did. He'd given her a week to calm down and during that week Nic had realised how much he loved her and he needed her in his life. His heart ached from the emptiness of not being with Gia. If she loved him back even a fraction as much as he loved her, he was prepared to take on the risk of a relationship. Now he could understand his father. Having loved and lost his wife was better than living an empty life filled with business and never having loved at all. But the cold hatred in Gia's eyes when she had told him she never wanted to see him again wouldn't leave him. He'd lain awake for nights and her face was imprinted on his mind.

I must see her. He had to convince her. Nic couldn't stand to think that she thought so little of herself and by trying to help her he had destroyed her passion—her belief in herself and her art. He wouldn't be able to live with himself.

Gia's cottage was locked up and there was no sign of her in the fields nearby. He knew without looking far that she was not there. She'd never once locked the door in the glorious weeks he'd stayed with her.

He drove to the restaurant but he was too early. It wasn't open. There was nowhere else to go but her family's house. Nic parked the car at the edge of the village and walked to the familiar house. A curtain twitched upstairs as he crossed the road and knocked on the door.

No answer. All was quiet. He stepped back and looked up, but the curtain was in place. As he walked around to the back of the house, he was met by voices. Mauro and his wife were sitting in the courtyard. As Gia's father caught sight of Nic, he stood and gestured for his wife to go inside. Nic walked over to the table.

'Mauro. *Signore* Carelli.' He looked at the man who stood staring at him without speaking. 'Is Gia here?'

'No. She is not.' Mauro's voice was cold.

'Will you tell me where I can find her?'

Before he could answer, Gabriel stepped down from the back of the house. Where Mauro's voice was cold and controlled, her brother's voice was loud.

'Why is he here?' He gestured rudely with a flick of his head before he addressed Nic. 'You are not welcome in our house or our village, so leave.'

'I want to speak to Gia. I want to make sure she is all right.'

'She is fine. She is happy without you.' Gabriel took Nic's arm and shook his fist in his face. 'You leave her alone, you hear me? I listened to you , and still you have broken my sister's heart.'

Nic stared at him before he looked down at the hand gripping his arm. 'If you can assure me without lying that she is all right, I will leave.'

Both men stared at him. 'Gia is fine.'

Nic turned on his heel and left.

***

It didn't take much for Nic to decide that he would stay at Carrara for another month. Antonio was happy running the company from Florence and Nic buried himself in his work now that the export deal was finalised. He negotiated more contracts for Baldini marble in four weeks than he had for the entire year before he'd met Gia. Occasionally, he managed to block her from his mind for hours at a time. He stayed away from the apartment in Florence because he didn't want to look at her landscapes every time he went there. The night he had come home from Castellina, he'd hauled Antonio over and they'd hung them in every room. Except for the one Gia had put her foot through. He'd sat that one against the wall in his bedroom to remind himself what a fool he'd been to lie to her.

Then he decided he couldn't bear to look at any of them, so he stayed in the apartment in Carrara on weekends.

Finally, his time at Carrara was finished. The staff was relieved. Nic knew he'd been tough to get on with and two secretaries had left in the past four weeks. Okay, so it was out of character for Mr Nice Guy to be such a bastard, but damn it, he had nothing to be happy about. It was time to pull the pin and go back to Florence. Just before five o'clock on his last afternoon, his father walked into Nic's office and closed the door behind him.

Nic stood. 'Papa. You should have said you were driving up.' He gripped the side of the desk as his father stared at him. 'Don't worry, everything's in place for the handover.'

'Sit down, Nic.' His father pulled out the chair on the other side of the desk and ran his hand through his short-cropped grey hair. Nic recognised the gesture. It was the same one he used when he was unsure of himself.

'I wanted to come . . . to come and tell you what a fine job you have done up here at Carrara for the past two years.'

Nic almost had to hold his mouth shut as he stared at his father.

'You did a fine job of salvaging those contracts with the Campbells, and I have seen how hard you have worked, even more so these last four weeks.'

Nic finally found his voice. 'Thank you.'

'I also wanted to tell you—' His father's voice shook.

'Tell me what?'

'How proud I am of the work you do. The children's hospital, the young artists, the appointment to the Uffizi'—he caught Nic's eye and his father's face split into a rare smile—'even though I don't understand this art stuff, I'm proud of you.' He lowered his voice. 'And your mother would have been too. Just don't let it consume you at the expense of your happiness.'

His father stood and held out his hand, and Nic reached over and shook it. 'I'll try not to.'

'Are you sure about the move back to Florence?' Antonio handed Nic a beer later that night. 'I thought you preferred to live out of the city.' Nic had driven back to Florence and met him at Antonio's favourite restaurant, despite Nic's insistence that he preferred to eat in.

'I used to.' Nic considered the crowd in the piazza below them. And then he'd remembered that being in Florence and eating in meant spending time in the apartment where Gia's landscapes covered the walls. They'd eat out. He'd sleep at the apartment and fill his days with business, and his nights and weekend at the gallery. His painting didn't even enter his thoughts. The one time he gave it any consideration was to decide to let it go completely.

'So, what happened in Tuscany?' Antonio looked at Nic over the top of his glass.

'Nothing.' Nic still didn't want to talk about it. He'd moved on. Or he'd tried his damned best to, but no one had told that to his subconscious who filled his dreams with Gia every night.

'Nic!' He lifted his head at the familiar voice and frowned. 'We haven't seen you out for ages.' It was Jolie, the journalist he'd hired to interview Gia.

'Jolie.' He kissed both of her cheeks, introduced Antonio, and gestured to a vacant seat at their table.

'We've missed you around town. The word is you're back for good now.' The interest and the wide eyes did nothing for him. After a few moments of desultory chat, Jolie stood to leave.

'I went to Castellina last week. I wanted to catch up with that friend of yours I interviewed. Such a shame.'

Nic's head flew up. He'd only been paying half attention to Jolie, and Antonio had kept the conversation rolling. 'A shame? What happened?'

'You can pick them, but—'

'What are you talking about?' His voice was cold. Jolie could be a bitch when she didn't get the attention she wanted.

'Gia Carelli has given up painting and the studio is closed. Such a waste. I had such great hopes for her. My goodness, Nic, you surely do have a perfect eye! It's such a pity that the talent you find can't ever seem to hold up to the pressure.'

Nic stood and pushed his chair back and nodded to Antonio. 'I'll see you before I go.'

Nic bolted from the restaurant and went back to the apartment. He poured himself a scotch and sat on the cold marble floor of the foyer and made himself look at Gia's work. Every time he wanted to close his eyes and push the memories away, he forced his eyes to stay open and he stared at the landscapes. He could hear her laugh. He could feel her hands on him, her breath against his face. The fragrance of the strawberry stuff she used on her hair. The smell of turpentine on her hands. When he pictured the tattoo he had painted on her breasts, Nic groaned and put his glass aside, dropping his head into his hands.

Selfish. He had been a selfish idiot. He had taken Gia's passion for her art like a leech and transferred it to himself.

And ironic. The Uffizi had chosen him for the vacancy

on the Board before he'd even met Gia, and he'd done his damn best to use her to get what he already had. He would never be a true artist like she was. His passion was for business and he had taken hers and tried to take it on as his own. Sure, he could paint, but so could many others. Being a true artist like Gia, and emotionally invested in your creation, was a rare gift, and he was personally responsible for killing that. Everything she had said about him was right. He had no understanding of her love for art. He had no understanding of giving up control and letting things take their course. He had no understanding of love and having someone in his life, even if it meant the risk of losing her. He was a coward.

All the energy he'd put into deals. All the energy he'd put into his charities. All he wanted to do was put that energy into Gia and make her realise that her talent should not be thrown away because of his selfish actions.

She was his perfect deal. And in all the right ways. He loved her—for who she was and what she brought to his life.

God damn it. He would convince her of that even if it meant camping outside her parents' house or the restaurant in Castellina—or wherever she lived these days— until she believed in herself . . . and his love for her.

Chapter Twenty-Two

Gia hated waiting tables. She hated customers. She hated the sight of food and most of all she hated the way her family treated her as though she was a fine piece of porcelain about to smash into a thousand pieces.

When Papa was in the kitchen or at the till, Gabriel took over and hovered over her. When they were upstairs, Mamma or Louisa fussed around her.

'Don't put that dish on that buffet; take it to the other one. Make sure the water is not too cold, the tourists like it warmer.' And then the personal stuff. 'Gia, have you had lunch today?'

Yada yada yada. It went on every hour of every day and then again at night. Telling her what to think and how to feel. The worst part was . . . she let them do it. Gia's shell grew thicker every day and their words began to fall on deaf ears. They talked and she managed to block it all out as she went about setting tables, serving food, and clearing tables.

Day in. Day out, Night in. Night out. The only thing she couldn't ignore was when Papa began to criticise Nic, which he seemed to do every week or so. It was all dredged up afresh and she had to listen to it.

'You made a mistake, *cara*.' His booming voice followed from the kitchen as she came in and out with orders. A little spark of life stirred.

Tell the world, Papa. It was Friday night and extra busy as the summer drew to a close. The Florentines were making the most of the last warm weather of the season.

'Yes, Papa.' Her voice was without expression. She'd had plenty of time to practise that over the past month. 'I know. I was very foolish. I did.'

Gia put her head down, collected the next meals and took them out to the courtyard. Of course, the customers were sitting at the table she thought of as Nic's table.

She knew he'd been trying to help her in his way. She knew his heart was giving. It was just that he had gone about it the wrong way. If only they could have talked about it when she'd calmed down. But she had driven Nic away without giving him a chance to explain—the same as her family did to her.

The day Nic had come to the house and she had watched him from behind the curtain, she had come so close to running down to see him, but Mamma had held her back.

And like the fool she was, Gia had listened and done as she was told, as always. The next day she moved back to her cottage, but her brushes and canvases remained locked away. The only time she let herself feel was when she looked at the painting she had done for Nic.

Without her art to absorb her energy, and without Nic to love, sometimes she felt like she was going to burst. But every comment, every criticism from her well-meaning family, she wore like a punishment.

She cleared some empty plates from the buffet table and carried them to the kitchen. As she waited for Gabriel to step aside and let her through, he frowned at her.

'Gia, why did you clear those plates away?'

'Because they were empty.' She looked down at them.

'You should have started from the other side where most of the tables are filled.' Gabriel shook his head and spoke softly just so Gia could hear. 'I don't know why you bother coming to work here. Unless I tell you what to do, you cannot get it right. You need to find yourself a husband and let him look after you. Someone quiet who can put up with your temperament.'

Gia's world shifted. All of the emotion she had refused to feel over the past four weeks exploded in one single burst.

She looked at her brother and her first words were deathly quiet as she held up one plate. 'This plate, Gabriel?

This was the wrong plate?'

'Yes.' He frowned and looked over her shoulder, distracted as someone came in the door behind her, but Gia ignored the new customers.

Gia held the plate up high and dropped it to the floor and it smashed to pieces on the tiles. Mou Mou skittered out from beneath the table and ran for the door with a loud yowl.

'And what about this one, Gabe? Is this the wrong one, too?' She held it even higher and threw it onto the floor as well before she whipped her apron off. The chatter of the patrons stopped and the restaurant was deathly silent as eyes widened. Gia picked up a third plate from the table beside her; she was beginning to enjoy herself. She could *feel.* For the first time in weeks, she could see the colours around her and smell the fragrance of the roses drifting in from the courtyard. But with feeling came pain and her heart ached, but she welcomed the pain.

Papa came running down from upstairs as Gia turned to Gabriel. His eyes were wide with shock. She held up a hand and he took a step back, but she followed, poking him in the chest. It felt so good.

'My temperament?' she shouted. 'What the hell do you know about my temperament? Just because I choose to paint my emotions doesn't mean I don't have them. I am more than capable of making love to a man all night until he begs for mercy, and I would crush a quiet husband with a single ounce of my passion.'

Oh yes, she was out to shock them.

To destroy their illusions of her once and for all. 'I do not need you to tell me what I want or deserve. And you do not have the right to put down Nic. No one knows more than I do what it's like to want to run away from expectations. I'm an *idiota* for letting you all bully me into giving up my painting and devoting my life to waitressing.'

Papa and Gabriel were joined by her sister, Louisa, and Mamma who had come from the kitchen to see what the noise was. She stared at her whole family lined up in front of her. 'I'm not even any good at it! But I'm an even bigger *idiota* for letting someone I love more than my art go without telling him how I feel.'

Gabriel opened his mouth and pointed behind her. 'Nic is— '

Gia raised her finger and poked her brother in the chest for the second time. 'Do not say one word against him. He is a good and kind man and I will forever regret not giving him a chance to explain things to me. He meant well.' She tossed her apron to the floor. 'Actually, I'm not living in the shadows anymore. I'm going to go after him.' She stared back at her family whose mouths were all hanging open. 'Right. Now.'

Gia twirled around.

'Oh *dio*,' she said as a smile crept over her face.

Nic stood in the doorway, grinning like an *idiota* as small pieces of china filled the floor around his feet. Gia looked around. Every head in the restaurant was turned to them and the people at the farthest tables were standing so they could see what was happening. Gia turned back to Nic, but he ignored her and stepped forward. Gia kept her eyes fixed on him as he walked past her and stood before her father.

'Mauro.' The sound of his beautiful voice sent tremors down Gia's back. 'May I ask for your daughter's hand in marriage?'

Gia's heart stopped beating as she watched her father and waited for his reply. Not that it mattered, she knew what she wanted. He nodded and put his arm around Mamma as she lifted her red and white apron to her face and burst into tears.

Nic turned around and lifted Gia's apron from the floor and used it to push the broken china aside and then he dropped to one knee, taking one of her hands in his. With his other hand, he reached into his pocket and removed a small box and flicked it open. A ring with a huge scarlet stone nestled in white satin.

You could have heard a pin drop. Every eye was fixed on them.

He held her gaze and his blue eyes looked at her full of love and honesty. 'Gia, my love. Will you marry me?'

Gabriel stepped forward and opened his mouth and Gia held up her other hand to stop him from speaking.

I really should have learned to do that years ago. It would have saved the whole family a lot of grief.

She smiled at her family as Gabriel stepped back before she turned to Nic. 'Of course, I will, Nic Baldini. What took you so long to come back?'

Gia stepped into his arms and Nic's lips found hers as a cheer went up around them.

***

Nic insisted on taking Gia back to Florence but she made him call in at the cottage on the way so she could give him the painting she had done. He had gripped her hand tightly when she had led him into her bedroom and shown him the only other painting he hadn't seen.

'I love it. And I love you.'

Now they stood in the foyer of his apartment, where he had hung it beside the others. Gia looked around. She was home.

Surrounded by her work, and in Nic's arms.

'You know I had to pay an outrageous amount to keep these paintings? Ben had to keep putting up the price because he could have sold them ten times over at your exhibition.' Nic touched his forehead to hers. 'I had to have them. Not because I didn't think you could carry the show, but because they were a part of you I couldn't bear to let go.'

Nic's fingers hovered over the top button of her blouse but Gia placed her hand on her hip and stepped back.

'I want you to promise you will never lie to me again.' Strength and belief in herself laced her words.

Nic unbuttoned the top button of her blouse. His breath brushed her cheek as he began to speak but Gia stepped back and held up one hand.

'No.' She shook her head slowly. 'I want your promise first.'

Nic grinned at her and dropped his hand. Gia looked down at hers with a grin. 'So, the hand works on you, too.' The power of her love filled her and she revelled in her happiness.

'I promise never to lie to you again.' He lifted his eyes back to hers and his expression was serious.

Gia didn't have to try hard for the sexy smile on her lips. 'Excellent. Because I'd hate to have to try plate throwing to get your attention. I'd much rather save my passion for the bedroom.'

Nic's lips left a trail of fire down Gia's neck as his own hands got busy on her buttons. 'And your paintings,' he murmured against her throat.

'Yes, and my paintings,' she said.

Gia waited until Nic lifted his head. 'I love you, Nic. I love you so much.'

'Of course, you do. I never doubted it. Oh, and I forgot to tell you, you will have to get busy.'

'Busy?' she asked with a frown.

'Painting. We are going to New York. I have negotiated an exhibition for you next summer.'

Gia squealed as Nic scooped her into his arms and strode across the marble-floored foyer. 'But most importantly, my dearest Gia, let me show you to *our* bedroom and then you can practise some of that passion.'

THE END

Acknowledgments

I would like to make special mention of Minerva Education, Cajsa J., and Pier Baldini, (no relation to Nic of my story) for the opportunity of attending the workshop in Tuscany with Eloisa James in the summer of 2014 and for introducing me to the wonderful Tuscan countryside and the village of Castellina-in-Chianti.

About the Author

Annie lives in Australia, on the beautiful north coast of New South Wales. She sits in her writing chair and looks out over the tranquil Pacific Ocean.

She writes contemporary romance, outback crime and historical romance. She loves telling stories that always have a happily ever after. She lives with her very own hero of many years and they share their home with Toby, the naughtiest dog in the universe, and Barney, the rag doll puss, who hides when the four grandchildren come to visit.

Stay up to date with her latest releases at her website: http://www.annieseaton.net

If you would like to stay up to date with Annie's releases, subscribe to her newsletter here: http://www.annieseaton.net

All Annie's books are available in eBook and print.

Direct eBook links:

https://www.annieseaton.net/ebook-store.html

They are also available from all eBook providers.

Click on the titles here:

https://www.annieseaton.net/all-books.html

Print Store:

All books are available in print at Annie's store

With FREE postage

https://annieseatonstore.ecwid.com/

Look for Annie's bestselling new series:
THE AUGATHELLA GIRLS

Awards

Finalist (Larapinta) - Book of the Year, Long Romance, RWA Ruby awards, 2023.

Book of the Year (Whitsunday Dawn) - Ausrom Readers' Choice Awards, 2018.

Finalist (Whitsunday Dawn) – ARRA romantic suspense 2019

Finalist - NZ KORU award, 2018 and 2020.

Winner - Best Established Author of the Year 2017, AUSROM.

Longlisted - Sisters in Crime Davitt Awards 2016, 2017, 2018, 2019, 2021, 2022, 2023.

Finalist (Kakadu Sunset) - Book of the Year, Long Romance, RWA Ruby awards, 2016.

Winner - Best Established Author of the Year, 2015 AUSROM.

Winner - Author of the Year 2014, AUSROM